William Gilbert

**The magic Mirror :**

a round of Tales for young and old

William Gilbert

**The magic Mirror :**
*a round of Tales for young and old*

ISBN/EAN: 9783337024901

Printed in Europe, USA, Canada, Australia, Japan

Cover: Foto ©Andreas Hilbeck / pixelio.de

More available books at **www.hansebooks.com**

ALEXANDER STRAHAN, PUBLISHER
LONDON AND NEW YORK
1866

# CONTENTS.

# I.

## THE GLASS BRAIN.

Towards the middle and latter end of the fifteenth century, there lived in Bishopsgate Street, London, a merchant of the name of Walter de Courcey. He was, at the time of our narrative, between forty-five and fifty years of age. In person he was a tall, well-built, powerful man; his face was not only handsome, but indicative of great intellectual power. In

disposition he was honourable, enterprising, and generous; but these good qualities were to a certain extent neutralised by haughtiness of manner, ambition, and a strong tendency towards despotism over those beneath him. His commercial transactions were, perhaps, greater than those of any merchant in the city of London, and he had the reputation of

B

possessing enormous wealth.   His house was magnificently furnished, and his hospitality corresponded
with his reputation for riches.   He was a widower,
with one daughter, at this time about nineteen years
of age.

In person, Bertha de Courcey strongly resembled
her father, the softness of the feminine characteristics

being at the same time well pre-
served.   She was handsome, yet
somewhat stern in countenance.
She had a fine forehead, bright
black eyes, a well-formed nose,
and a mouth garnished with a
beautiful set of teeth.   Her form
was tall and exceedingly graceful, slender without being thin,
majestic but still not heavy.
She was now residing with a
maternal aunt in Calais, but her return home was
almost daily expected by her father.

Of all the different countries with which Master
Walter de Courcey traded, his transactions with
Venice were the greatest.   Indeed, his business with
that city exceeded that of any other merchant in
England.   And as Venice at that time was the principal port of communication with the East, it naturally followed that Master Walter had vast quantities
of valuable goods, jewels, and rich stuffs sent to him
by his correspondents.   Indeed, his agent in Venice
had orders to forward him whatever was valuable,

and at the same time new and uncommon, to adorn the rooms of his own mansion.

But there was one article of luxury after which Master Walter especially sighed, of which he had heard a great deal, but which he had not seen, and that was a glass mirror. He had not only seen, but he also possessed several of the largest metal mirrors in England. They might be found in his rooms, both of silver and a baser metal composed of tin and copper; but according to all accounts they were not to be compared in beauty to those made of glass at Venice. Glass mirrors had lately been invented, and a manufactory for them had been established at Murano near Venice; but as it was in the hands of the Venetian government, who were extremely jealous of their secret, and as they generally presented the mirrors made at their manufactory to crowned heads, as gifts of great price, it was extremely difficult for the English merchant, rich as he was, to obtain one.

At last, his correspondent in Venice wrote to him that a Venetian nobleman, who would be especially recommended to him, was shortly about to visit England. The nobleman, he wrote, would bring with him a magnificent mirror of the description Master Walter so much coveted, but what he intended doing with it no one knew. He was, the correspondent continued, a very singular man; some said he was partially insane, while others considered him an expert in the black art. Of one thing he particularly advised Master Walter, and that was not to make the nobleman, who was extremely proud, an offer in money for his mirror, as it would probably offend him. The better plan would be, when he presented his letter of introduction, to offer him the hospitality of his house, and then Master Walter could take his own opportunity of ingratiating himself in his favour; and it was very possible that the precious object which wealth could not purchase might thereupon be offered as a mark of gratitude and esteem.

It may easily be imagined that the sturdy English feeling of Master Walter revolted at the scheme proposed by his wily Italian correspondent; he nevertheless determined that his visitor should have no reason to complain of any want of hospitality. He fitted up a magnificent suite of apartments for his reception, and hired several experienced servants who could speak Italian to attend upon him, and then somewhat impatiently awaited his arrival. At last an avant-courier announced his approach, and a few hours afterwards the Count Vicenzio Garavaglia arrived. Master Walter no sooner heard the horses' feet in the courtyard than he descended to welcome his guest. A footman drew the curtains of the litter aside, and by the light of the torches Master Walter perceived the Count, who addressed him in perfect English as he raised himself with difficulty on his elbow.

"Excuse me, Master Walter, if I do not rise to receive you, but you see before you a great invalid.

A terrible malady has seized me, from which I am afraid I shall never recover. I have many apologies," he continued, "to offer you for the trouble and inconvenience I am about to give you, but I am sure, from the description I have heard of you from your Venetian correspondent, that you have sufficient charity to forgive me."

Master Walter immediately expressed his great sorrow at his guest's misfortune, and assured him that his house was at his entire disposal, and every assistance he could render should be given.

"I expected no other from your kindness," said the Count.

Some of the Count's servants now advanced to take him from his litter, and to carry him up to his room, for he was too weak to mount the staircase without them. Master Walter then ordered his men to remove the Count's baggage into his room as speedily as possible. It consisted of several large travelling trunks, and a large case about six feet long and four feet broad, with a depth of perhaps eight inches, carefully bound with iron bands. Master Walter immediately guessed that this was the much-coveted mirror, but he had too much discretion to make any remark on the subject. When all had been carried up-stairs, he entered the house himself, and seating himself in the dining-room quietly remained till he should receive a message from his guest.

In about half an hour he was greatly surprised by seeing the Count enter the room leaning on two of his Italian servants. Master Walter had now a better opportunity of observing the person of his  guest than he had when he reclined in his litter. He was tall and miserably thin, and so weak that not-withstanding his sup-ports he could hardly move one leg after the other. His face was intensely pale, and his eyes deeply sunk in his head; yet his counte-nance was eminently handsome and intel-lectual. He wore a long thin black beard; his eyebrows were well-marked, and his fore-head high. His hair had disappeared from the front of his head, but apparently not from age, for he seemed hardly to exceed forty. His nose was high and somewhat curved, and altogether there was a slight Hebrew expression in his countenance. His hands and feet were small and beautifully made, and his whole appearance most prepossessing. All these advantages were heightened by the dress he wore. He was attired completely in black. He wore the close-fitting silk hose we see in the pictures of the old Venetian school, very loose trousers, which descended to the knee and were there fastened round the legs, a tight-fitting waistcoat, and over it a loose-flowing robe which reached to the calf of the leg. His dress, with the exception of his hose, was made of rich black velvet, and his robe was trimmed with a glossy dark sable. His neck was open, his collar being fastened by a buckle consisting of one magnificent diamond, the only ornament he wore on his person.

Master Walter rose to receive his guest, and assisted him to a seat by the fire. As soon as the servants had retired, the Count addressed his host:

"I am really inexpressibly sorry at the inconvenience I am about to put you to; but I would willingly relieve you of my presence if I could. You see before you the wreck of a man who has but a few days to live. I will, however, endeavour to render your abode as little mournful as I can. For the future I will not speak of my illness, and you will greatly oblige me if you do not. I wish as far as I can to conceal the state I am in, and each time you mention it, it will give me another grief at the certainty of the trouble I am about to cause you."

Master Walter merely remarked that he hoped his guest was deceived in the view he had taken of his malady; and the conversation turned on other subjects.

"I understand," said the Count Garavaglia, "that you have a charming daughter; I trust I shall have the pleasure of making her acquaintance."

"It will give both my daughter and myself great pleasure. She is now absent, but I expect her arrival to-morrow or next day at the latest. In the meantime let me know if I can be of any service to you in London."

"You can be of great service to me," said the Count; "but I hardly like to tell you in what way."

"Why not?"

"I am afraid the commission I should give you would be little to your taste; but should you decline to execute it, I am sure I may trust to your discretion, to reveal to no one the request I am about to make to you. In London there resides a merchant of the name of Mendez. I will not disguise from you that he is a member of the Jewish persuasion, although he conceals his faith, as his nation is in little favour with you. I much wish to see that man."

"I know him well," said Master Walter, "and a most honourable man he is. I have long suspected his religious persuasion, but of course I never mentioned my suspicion to him. To-morrow morning I will send a messenger to him, and I am sure you will see him in the course of the day; that is to say, if he be the man I think."

"I have here," said the Count, "a letter to him with his address on it, perhaps that will assist you."

Master Walter having glanced at the address found it was the merchant of whom he had spoken.

The conversation was now interrupted by some servants, who came in to arrange the table for supper.

"I do not know," said Master Walter, "whether our English kitchen will meet your taste; I am afraid not. However, for the future, if you will tell me how I can alter it to make it more to your liking I will take care it shall be done."

"In that respect," said the Count smiling, "I shall be fortunate enough to spare you all trouble. In my weak state of health I am obliged to be very particular in my diet, and I have brought with me a cook of my own. He has all his implements along with him, and can cook the little I want without interfering with the arrangements of your servants."

He had hardly concluded when one of the Count's servants entered the room, carrying with him a silver bowl which contained some soup, and a small velvet cap, which he offered to his master.

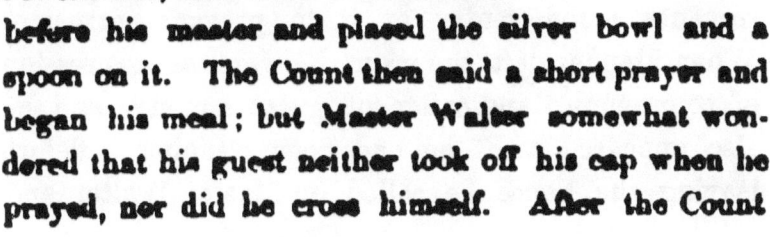

" Will you excuse me if I wear my cap?" said he to Master Walter; " I am afraid of the draught of air in the room, comfortable as it is."

The servant, whose expression of countenance was of a strongly Jewish cast, then drew a small table before his master and placed the silver bowl and a spoon on it. The Count then said a short prayer and began his meal; but Master Walter somewhat wondered that his guest neither took off his cap when he prayed, nor did he cross himself. After the Count had tasted a few spoonfuls he beckoned his servant, who immediately took away the bowl and removed the table to its place. Master Walter, who was taking his supper at the large table, again noticed that the Count murmured a short prayer without uncovering his head or crossing himself. Somewhat scandalised at his guest's irreverent manner, Master Walter, who was a pious Catholic, continued his supper but made no remark. A short time afterwards the Count, pleading great fatigue, took leave of his host, and two of the foreign servants assisted their master out of the room.

Early the next morning Walter de Courcey dispatched a messenger to the merchant Mendez, who was fortunately at home. He appeared greatly surprised to hear the Count had arrived, and sent word back he would wait upon him about noon. Master Walter in the meantime descended to his counting-house and warehouse, and was soon absorbed in his business.

When Mendez arrived he was ushered into the Count's bedroom, where he remained closeted with him for more than an hour. On what subjects they conversed it is impossible to say. The door of the room was closed the while, and one of the foreign servants stood sentry at it to prevent intrusion. When Mendez left the room he wore an expression of countenance indicative of great anxiety, and he also appeared as if he had been weeping. Before leaving the house he called on Master Walter and

expressed his sorrow at the trouble the invalid was
giving him, but he said it would last but a short
time, as it was utterly impossible he could live a
week.

Master Walter, on his part, deplored the ill-health
of his guest, and attempted to draw from Mendez
some particulars respecting him, but in vain. Mendez,
while wearing an appearance of great obsequious-
ness and seemingly desirous to oblige, evaded all
questions; and Master Walter, finding he could obtain
no information from him, discreetly dropped the
conversation.

That evening Bertha, Master Walter's daughter,
returned from France, and great indeed was her
father's joy at seeing her. During the months
she had been absent she had greatly improved in
appearance, and was really a very beautiful girl. The
Count did not make his appearance that evening,
his servant excusing him on the plea that he felt
much weaker.

As soon as the servant had left the room, Master
Walter related to his daughter all the particulars he
knew about his guest. Bertha took but little interest
in the matter till the mirror was spoken of, and then
her curiosity was excited to the highest degree.
Although little accustomed as yet to mix with the
world, the news of the wonderful invention had
reached her, and when she understood there was
one in the house, great was her anxiety to see it
and prove its powers. Her father told her it was

impossible, as the Count was at present too ill to be troubled on the subject, but the young lady mentally determined that it should be from no want of exertion on her part if she did not succeed. She now inquired many particulars about the Count, and finding from her father's description that he was a most courteous gentlemanly man, she determined on making an attack upon him as soon as she should see him. She then went to bed, revolving in her mind in what way she could make, her application in the most irresistible manner possible.

The next morning both father and daughter, when breakfasting together, conversed principally on family matters, but the subject of the mirror continually occupied the minds of both. The only remark that was made about it was by the young lady, who inquired if the case containing it was to be opened that morning, as she should like to be present on the occasion.

"I do not think it likely, my dear," her father replied; "however, if the Count orders the case to be opened, I will be sure to inform you. I much fear, however, he is too unwell to occupy himself with such matters."

He had hardly done speaking when a messenger arrived from the Count.

He had sent to inquire after the health of his host, and also that of his daughter, whose arrival he had heard of, and also to say that he personally felt somewhat better that morning, and if he continued so till

the evening he would do himself the pleasure to wait
upon Master Walter de Courcey. At the same time
he would crave permission to be exempted from
attending the family meals, as well as to be allowed
to have his food cooked in his own rooms.

Of course all this was willingly accorded, and
the messenger left.

During that day nothing occurred particularly
worthy of record. As the evening approached Miss
Bertha began to occupy herself with her toilet. She
was beautiful and she knew it, and she was determined to make as favourable an impression on the
Count as she could, with the view of being allowed
to see the wonderful mirror. She had hardly
joined her father five minutes in the saloon, when
the Count was led in by his two servants. He
seemed weaker than he was on the night of his
arrival; still his appearance was most prepossessing,
and his courteous salutation and manner made a
great impression on the young lady. She really
sympathised with him,—a circumstance somewhat
rare with her, as she was naturally intensely selfish,
—and for the moment forgot all about the mirror.
As the evening advanced, however, and the Count's
strength rallied a little, the conversation took a
livelier turn, and Bertha, with great tact, turned
it on the subject of the new invention of glass
mirrors, and asked if it were true that in point of
excellence those of Venice exceeded all others.

"Nothing can be more true, young lady," he said.

"Even I, accustomed as I have daily been to the sight of them since they were first invented, am still surprised at their wonderful powers when I see them."

"And in what," said Bertha, "are these mirrors so superior to all others? I have one of silver in my chamber which appears to me to be as clear as it is possible to make one."

"I have no doubt," said the Count, "that your mirror is as perfect as it is possible for a silver mirror to be, but still it is far inferior to those of Venetian glass. I will endeavour to explain it to you. From the position you are now in, you see the whole of the room before you clearly and distinctly enough. Suppose now my mirror were placed in front of you, the whole of your person as well as the back part of the room would be as distinct as that part of the room you now see, the colours perfect, the distance properly kept, and in fact it would simply appear to you that you were looking into another apartment in which there was sitting a perfect image of yourself, so accurately presented that you would almost doubt the reality of your presence in the spot you are now in."

"And you can have the heart," said Bertha, almost reproachfully, "to keep a treasure of the kind fast nailed up in a wooden case?"

"My dear young lady," replied the Count, "remember that, although I have always a great pleasure in seeing it, it is not the wonderful curiosity to me that it is to others. Nevertheless, it is my intention to open it in a few days, if Heaven allows me to live so long, and then I shall have it always before me when I am in my chamber."

"I do not wish it for myself," said Bertha, now almost in despair, "but I heard my father say how much he should like to see it. Perhaps, when you open the case, you would allow him to be present?"

Master Walter almost imperceptibly raised his eyebrows in surprise, but said nothing.

"I shall be most happy to oblige your father," said the Count; "still I hope he will allow me to put it off for a few days. I am sure he will offer no objection. A merchant so occupied with immense affairs of his own, I am sure, will not be impatient about such a really trifling subject, in comparison, as a looking-glass."

Master Walter merely said he should have much pleasure in waiting the perfect convenience of his guest.

Bertha now fairly bit her lips with vexation, which was increased by her noticing a certain arch expression on the features of the Count, not amounting to a smile, but something closely approaching it.

"I hope," she said at last, "you will also allow me to be present at the opening of the case. I assure you that great as is my father's curiosity to behold it, it is trifling to mine."

"That is a very different affair, my dear young lady," said the Count. "Why did you not say so before? I would willingly oblige you in every way in my power. I promise you that to-morrow, about noon, the case shall be opened, if I am strong enough to be present, which, for certain reasons I will then explain, is absolutely necessary. You shall be informed when it takes place, and I trust you will be pleased with my mirror when you see it."

The next day at noon Bertha sent to her father in the counting-house and reminded him of his appointment with the Count. Master Walter returned with the messenger, and found his daughter on the tiptoe of expectation; but he somewhat disappointed her by requesting she would remain in the dining-room till he had first visited his guest, as possibly he might not be prepared to receive her. The precaution was not in vain; for Master Walter found the Count in bed, and in a lamentably weak state. He was, however, most courteously received.

"I am, unfortunately, not able to perform my promise," he said; "in fact, I fear it will be out of my power altogether to be present at the opening of the mirror, for I feel my end is rapidly approaching. I can easily perceive that both you and your daughter would be highly pleased to possess the mirror, and as I wish to leave you some mark of my gratitude for the kindness I have received at your hands, pray consider it as a legacy from me to you. Giacomo," he continued, addressing his head servant, " remember, after my death, the mirror belongs to Master Walter. I should inform you, however," he said, turning his head to the merchant, " that a mystery is attached to it, which

renders the possession of it by no means the treasure you imagine, at least to those who do not follow the advice inscribed upon it. To the contented mind there is no danger whatever. I am, however, too weak to give you its history to-day; call on me to-morrow, and I will inform you of all. Without any discourteous wish on my part, pardon me if I say I have present need of sleep. Do not fail to see me to-morrow; in the meantime commend me to your fair daughter."

Master Walter, after thanking the Count warmly for his liberality, left him to his repose.

Bertha was obliged to bear her disappointment as

she best could, which was certainly not in a very amiable manner. There was, however, no alternative; and she impatiently waited for the morrow, when there might still be an opportunity for her to see the mirror.

Next morning the Count was no more. He had expired in the night, and his servants were employed in placing him in his coffin when Master Walter paid his visit. Outside the bedroom door was seated Mendez on the floor, with rent garments, after the manner of the Jews. He, however, rose when he saw Master Walter approach, and, with tears in his eyes, informed him of the death of the Count. He, moreover, requested permission to remove the body that night, that he might make preparations for sending it back to Italy, where it was to be buried. He further said, if it would not be inconvenient to Master Walter, he would, at the same time, remove the whole of the Count's effects, with the exception of the mirror, which, being Master Walter's property, was to remain. The merchant on his side had no objection to offer, and at a late hour the same night the body of the Count, as well as the whole of his baggage, was delivered over to Mendez, who a few days later left London, and never afterwards returned to it.

The next morning Master Walter de Courcey sent for his daughter to be present at the opening of the case containing the mirror. Bertha, who was at the moment in her chamber, was not slow in obeying the invitation, and both father and daughter proceeded together to a chamber near the one the Count had died in, and some men were sent to bring to them the case containing the mirror. A carpenter was present, who carefully undid the iron bands which bound the case, and took off the lid. Both father and daughter, as soon as they cast their eyes on the mirror, were struck speechless with astonishment. The men then raised it carefully from the ground, still in its case, and placed it upright. The mirror was of oval shape, of one entire piece of crystal. It was fixed in an exquisitely carved frame, so richly gilt that it appeared of solid gold.

There was, however, a singular peculiarity remarkable in it. On the top of the glass, just beneath the frame, and following its curve, were some characters or hieroglyphics embossed in ruby-coloured glass, so brilliant that they almost dazzled the eye to look on them. Of what language these letters were it was impossible to say; even Master Walter, who was an excellent linguist, knew nothing of them.

" It is really very magnificent," said Bertha.

" Beautiful, indeed," said her father.

But it is more than probable that the exclamations of father and daughter arose from two distinct sentiments. The merchant was simply struck with the exquisite clearness and transparency of the mirror; his daughter with the admirable manner in which it reflected her person.

" It appears almost too beautiful and pure for mortal hands to have made," said the merchant, examining it closely. "The diamond is as brilliant certainly; but I much doubt if its transparency is so pure. What a singular faculty to possess, that of having everything reflected truthfully upon it! To it there is no deception. The old may paint their wrinkles, but the mirror sees them. To it the beautiful are beautiful, and the deformed, deformed. If a man could only possess a faculty of this kind, of what immense service it would be to him !"

" How so, father?" said Bertha, totally indifferent, however, to the subject.

" Simply in having everything presented to him without disguise ; while he, calm, cool, and collected, utterly unimpressionable to external sensations, would clearly judge of the question before him."

" And what good would that do you, father ?"

" Good ! why I believe if my brain were made of crystal as pure as this, I should succeed in everything I attempted."

" But, dear father, how would that benefit you ?

At present you are one of the richest men in England, and what can you wish for more?"

"To be the richest, my dear. Yes, I sincerely wish my brain were made of glass as clear as that, and I would make you, my child, not only the wealthiest heiress in the world but also the most sought after."

Bertha merely laughed.

"But tell me, father," she said, "what the meaning is of those strange-shaped letters on the glass."

"I do not know, my dear."

"You do not know? You who speak so many languages?"

"No, in sad truth I do not, and I am somewhat vexed at it, for now I remember the Count said there was a mystery connected with the glass, and perhaps those characters might explain it."

"I think," said Bertha, "it was a very foolish idea to put letters on the mirror which none can understand."

"Perhaps, my dear," said her father, "they might contain, in the language of the country for which this mirror was made, some excellent piece of advice."

"But at any rate they are useless to us, whatever they may have been to others," said Bertha.

"Very true, my dear; shall I send the mirror back?" said the merchant, in a joking tone.

Bertha merely laughed and kissed her father, and

the two shortly afterwards left the room, the merchant carefully locking the door after him, that no mischief might happen to the mirror from the carelessness of servants.

Master Walter descended into his counting-house, and was soon occupied with his business affairs, so

much so as completely to forget the mirror for the moment. Not so Bertha: she retired to her chamber, and thought of nothing else. She had never appeared so beautiful in her own eyes as at the moment she saw herself reflected in it; and her image still remained on her mind. She considered also that she must appear to others as lovely as to herself; and if that were the case, what would ultimately be her lot? A nobleman or a prince might fall in love with her, and she might rise from being a merchant's daughter to be one of the proudest and noblest ladies in the land. Other things had occurred far more unlikely than that!

She continued in her chamber, building castles in the air, till it was time for Master Walter to return to

supper. The meal had been on the table some time
before he made his appearance, and when he did he
was so pale and haggard that his daughter asked
him if he were unwell.

"Never better," he replied, "my dear, with the
exception of a slight headache, and that I daresay
will go off after supper."

"Then something has occurred to annoy you," said
Bertha.

"Nothing of the kind, my dear; why do you
ask?"

"Because you look so pale and worried. I am
certain something has happened to make you
angry."

"And I am equally certain that nothing of the
kind has happened," said he, smiling faintly. "On
the contrary, everything to-day has gone on in a
most satisfactory manner—never more so. Not a
single thing has gone contrary to my wishes, and I
succeeded on 'Change in every bargain I made. I
never in a single day made so much money as I have
in this."

"And what do you intend doing with it?"

"Making it the dowry of a naughty troublesome girl," he answered, pulling her ear playfully
the while

They now sat down to their meal, for which, however, Master Walter appeared to have but little
appetite. This increased the anxiety of his daughter,
who, with all her natural selfishness, was tenderly

attached to her father. Very little conversation passed between them, and that only in short detached sentences.

"It must be very pleasant, father," said Bertha, "to make money so rapidly. You are very fortunate when so many have difficulty in getting sufficient for the bare necessaries of life."

"I ought to consider myself so, my child, but somehow to-night I hardly feel it."

"Why not?"

"I cannot tell, but I do not."

Another pause ensued.

"Should you not like to be Lord Mayor, father? With your standing in the City I should think it a very easy thing for you to be elected."

"Very likely, and I have often thought of it, and even wished it ardently; but the wish has passed away."

"You cannot be well to-night, my dear father; you have eaten nothing."

"I told you before, my dear, there is nothing the matter with me," he answered, somewhat petulantly; "do not say so again."

Bertha became silent, and her father sat moodily for some time, his head resting the while on his hand.

Bertha attempted two or three other sentences, but received only short answers, and she gave up the attempt. Presently her father rose from his chair.

" I feel somewhat tired, my dear," he said, with his usual kindness of tone when addressing his daughter,

"and shall go to bed." So saying, he kissed his child and left the room.

The next morning they met together at breakfast, but the merchant was as silent and moody as the night before. Bertha remembering his aversion to be questioned on his health, did not speak of it, although she could easily perceive from the manner in which he sat leaning his head on his hand that he was not well. Their meal over, he rose and left her, telling her he should not dine at home, but would meet her again at supper.

That morning, Master Walter, who was Alderman of his ward, had some business with the Lord Mayor in council, and he bent his steps to the Guildhall.

On arriving at the building, he found the constables, the City watch, and the Train-bands assembled in the courtyard. He watched them attentively for some time, especially remarking their dress, which was much faded and in bad condition. He spoke to no one on the subject, but entered the hall, apparently reflecting on something of great interest. When he had entered the Council Chamber he found the Lord Mayor had been sent for that morning by the King on some business of importance, and that the meeting of aldermen had been adjourned till the afternoon. After conversing for some time on indifferent subjects, he left the building, but on passing some of his brother aldermen he was much annoyed by hearing one say to another, "How pale and ill Master Walter appears this morning! I hope he is not going to be unwell, for he is one of the most useful men among us."

"I noticed that myself," said the other; "the expression of his countenance seems entirely changed. I hope there is nothing wrong with him either in body or mind, for as you very justly say we should miss him greatly."

Master Walter now hurried on 'Change, and there appeared to avoid all his acquaintances; but from the frequent glances he threw around him he was evidently looking for some person who was not there. Presently two foreign merchants, Flemings, made their appearance, and he immediately advanced towards them.

"Good morning, gentlemen," he said, "I am glad to see you have not yet left England."

"Many thanks," said the elder; "can I be of any service to you in Ghent, Master Walter? for we leave to-morrow."

"No, I thank you; at present I have no commissions there. May I ask what takes you away?"

"Simply that we can transact no business here, and we are only wasting our time."

"Is not that your own fault?" said Master Walter. "I am afraid it is rather from the high price you ask for your venture of cloth than any want of will on the part of the London merchants to purchase."

"You have not been rightly informed on the subject. The price we asked for the cloth was extremely moderate; so much so, that if we had sold it at the sum we last offered it at, we should have gained nothing by our own venture."

"I certainly, then," said Master Walter, "have been misinformed. I am sorry I did not know you offered it on such conditions, or I might have been tempted to become a purchaser, but it is too late now."

"I do not know that," said the Flemish merchant. "It is true we have re-shipped the whole, but if you would purchase the entire quantity we should be disposed to let you have it."

"Where is the ship?" said Master Walter.

"Opposite the Tower. If you would like to enter-

tain the question we could go there at once, and you
could see the cloth."

Master Walter said that as he had no other business on hand at the moment he would go with them,
and the three immediately walked down to Paul's
Wharf and took a boat to the Tower.

When they had arrived on board the ship, the
Flemish merchants ordered some of the bales of cloth

to be brought upon
deck, and they were
opened one after the
other, and Master
Walter examined the
quality attentively. He
then asked the mer-
chants what sum they
would take for their
venture, and after much
conversation he pur-

chased the whole, on condition that it should be
immediately sent to his warehouse in Bishopsgate,
where he would then pay them the full amount.
The Flemings readily accepted the conditions; the
goods were immediately unshipped; porters and
pack-horses were soon provided; and in less than
three hours all was safely housed in Master
Walter's warehouses, and the purchase-money
paid.

As soon as the Flemish merchants had left him,
Master Walter hastened to the Guildhall, where he

found the Lord Mayor and aldermen assembled in council.

"We are most happy to see you, Master Walter," said the Lord Mayor, when he perceived him enter. "We were afraid we should not have the benefit of your opinion. We are deliberating on a very serious subject. His Majesty the King has most graciously promised to honour the corporation with his presence at a dinner this day fortnight, and we wish to do credit to the City in the entertainment we shall offer him. It has been suggested that the liveries of the City watch should be new for the occasion, as well as the uniforms of the Train-bands; but we do not know where to purchase the cloth; no merchant that we can hear of having sufficient for the purpose. Can you advise us on the subject?"

"My lord," said Master Walter, "I can; but if I do, I am afraid you will think me somewhat selfish."

"How so?"

"I believe I am at this moment the largest holder of cloth in London; but I should not be disposed, even to do honour to his Majesty, to sell it to the corporation under its full value."

"At such a time and on such an occasion," said the Lord Mayor, "we cannot haggle about price. Tell us the quantity you have, and the sum you ask for it, and we will give you an answer."

Master Walter rapidly calculated the quantity and the price he had paid the Flemings. He doubled the amount of the money, and said that considering the present scarcity of cloth he could not feel justified in taking less.

The aldermen somewhat demurred, but at last, finding they could not do better, accepted the terms.

After the meeting had broken up, the Lord Mayor called Master Walter aside, and confided to him that he believed from the conversation he had had with his Majesty that morning there was a strong probability of a war with France, and also that he suspected his Majesty would request a loan of money from the City, and in that case he should much like Master Walter to advise him on the subject. Master Walter, in reply, said that his best endeavours should be given both to the corporation and his Majesty. The Lord Mayor then suggested that if the King should speak to him on the matter he should propose to introduce Master Walter to him, as being of all the aldermen the best capable of giving advice. Master Walter readily assented, and shortly afterwards he and the Lord Mayor parted.

Although it was growing late in the day, Master Walter did not go home, but went again on 'Change. He found but few merchants there, but among them was one he particularly wanted to see. This was Master Biffi, a Lombard merchant of great renown. Master Walter immediately accosted him, and asked him if he had any corselets of Milan steel, as he wished to purchase a few. Master Biffi informed him that he had received notice of a consignment of more than

a hundred, which he expected daily. He had two
or three corselets at his house of exactly the same
description, and if Master Walter would go with
him he would show them to him. Master Walter
accepted the invitation, and was much pleased with
those he saw. The price also was moderate, and he
not only bought them all, but entered into an agreement for the purchase of the whole number expected from Milan. The terms of the bargain
having been fully arranged, Master Walter left for
his own house.

It might naturally have been expected that after
so fortunate a day's work Master Walter would have
been in high good humour, but such was not the
case. He had that day netted a profit greater than
he had acquired in any one entire year since he had
been in business, yet it had not the slightest effect in
raising his spirits. He appeared perfectly callous to
the whole affair. When he entered his house, he
was exceedingly pale, though it was more the pallor
of ill-health than fatigue; yet he did not complain.
When his daughter entered the supper-room she was
somewhat alarmed on finding him seated in his chair
with his hand pressed on his brow. She kissed him
affectionately, and asked him after his health. He
replied that with the exception of a certain painless
heaviness of the head he was quite well. They sat
down to supper, but he ate nothing. He tasted
several dishes, but he immediately sent them away.
Bertha asked him where he had dined, and received for

answer that he had eaten nothing since he had left
the house in the morning.    Presently he entered
more freely into conversation, and recounted to her
the adventures of the day.    The girl was excessively
pleased at her father's good fortune, and expressed
herself warmly to that effect, but Master Walter
seemed perfectly indifferent to it.    They conversed
together for some time, and Bertha noticed the while
that he sat the whole time leaning his head on his
hand.    Later he rose from the table somewhat
abruptly, wished her good night, and left the room.

The next morning they met at breakfast: Master
Walter was as pale as the evening before, and silent
but not listless.    To his daughter's inquiries about
his health, he simply replied that he was quite well,
save the slight weight in the head, which would pro
bably go off in the course of the day.    He ate mode-
rately at breakfast, but evidently without appetite or
care for what was set before him.    When they had
finished their meal, Bertha asked him to come with
her to see the manner in which she had had the mirror put up in her sitting chamber, stating that it appeared now more beautiful than ever.    At the mention
of the mirror Master Walter looked for the moment
surprised, as if it had escaped his memory.    In fact,
although a few days before so anxious for its possession, he had now totally forgotten it, and when his
daughter had called his attention to it he felt not the
slightest interest in it.    To Bertha's invitation he
replied with much kindness of tone that he had no

doubt she had arranged it admirably well, but that he should not have time to go with her to see it, as he had promised to be with the Lord Mayor at an early hour.

"But, father," said Bertha, "I feel hurt you do not take more interest in what I have done. To oblige your daughter you might on such an occasion as this, I think, not only keep the Lord Mayor waiting, but the Court of Aldermen too."

"What occasion do you allude to, my dear?" said her father.

"My birthday," said Bertha, pouting. "I am nineteen to-day, father," she continued reproachfully. "This is the first time you have forgotten it."

"My dearest child," said Master Walter, "pray forgive me. I ought not to have forgotten it I own, but I am so overwhelmed with business that it entirely slipped from my memory. I really am very sorry, but let us go and see the mirror at once."

Although Master Walter said he was very sorry, and afterwards expressed his regret in still stronger terms, it was at the same time without the slightest sympathy in his tone; on the contrary, Bertha could hardly conceal from herself that he treated the matter with perfect indifference. When they arrived in the chamber in which Bertha had placed the mirror, Master Walter paid her the highest compliments on the taste she had shown in the arrangements, but his voice had the same cold artificial tone which she had noticed at the breakfast table.

"Bertha," he said at last, "this is your nineteenth birthday, and I intend making you a very handsome present; one, in fact, worthy of so excellent a daughter. From this day forward the mirror is your own. And now, my dear, I must go, but kiss me first."

Bertha kissed her father, and her eye followed him with some anxiety, not unmixed with mortification, as he left the room; for his manner when he presented her with the mirror was that of a man wishing to disembarrass himself of what he did not care to possess, rather than that of an affectionate father making his daughter a present on her birthday.

When Master Walter left the house, after giving directions in his warehouse to deliver the cloth he had purchased the day before from the Flemish merchants to any person the Court of Aldermen should authorise to receive it, he went direct to Guildhall, and had an interview with the Lord Mayor. His lordship informed him that he had just received an order from the King to attend him, and he requested Master Walter to accompany him.

"Candidly," said the Lord Mayor, who was an eminent fishmonger, "I am not quick at figures, and you are; and I know perfectly well that his Majesty wants me about the loan. I cannot introduce you to the King at once, but if you remain in one of the ante-rooms while I go in, I will mention your name when he begins to talk of money matters, and you will be sure to be sent for."

As they walked together to the palace, Master Walter spoke but little, and merely replied to his companion's remarks with monosyllables. The mission he was on suited his tastes admirably. We have already stated that he was exceedingly ambitious. He had always aspired to be in favour at the Court, and now he intuitively perceived that his wishes were on the point of being attained Nay, more, he was as certain that he should be courteously received by the King, and afterwards taken into his royal favour and confidence, as if the thing had already happened. And yet he felt neither pleasure nor satisfaction at the knowledge. It would annoy him immensely if it did not occur, and yet he felt no joy at the certainty of the fulfilment of his most ardent wishes.

They at last arrived at Crosby Palace, and were shown by the ushers into a waiting-room, while one went to inform the King of the Lord Mayor's attendance. He shortly afterwards returned, and taking his lordship with him he again left the room. When Master Walter was alone, he paced backwards and forwards in the room, somewhat wondering at his own apathy now his utmost ambition was on the point of being realised.

The Lord Mayor had been but a short time with the King before the usher entered the ante-room, and informed Master Walter that his Majesty required his attendance. Master Walter immediately obeyed, and the next moment found himself for the first time in his life in the presence of royalty. In the room were also the Prime Minister, the Lord Mayor, and two or three lords of the council. After the ceremony of introduction, the King said : "Master Walter, we have heard often of you, and always in terms of praise, and have now sent for you to advise us in our present strait. We have, for certain reasons I will not now explain, urgent need of money for the purposes of government, and we have applied to our faithful corporation of London for assistance. The Lord Mayor informs me he has no doubt our faithful citizens will assist us in our need, but, perhaps with too much modesty, tells us that others have more ability than himself in matters of finance, and especially pointed out to us yourself. I trust you will now aid us with your advice."

Master Walter of course readily promised the King every assistance in his power, and the King and his nobles immediately explained to him the case, and the security to be offered. It would be out of our province to relate the particulars, inasmuch as they have no bearing on our tale; suffice it to say, Master Walter spoke well and lucidly on the subject, and the King and the nobles were much pleased with him and complimented him highly.

"We were not aware," said his Majesty, "we had near us a man of so much ability. I am afraid we shall trouble you frequently for your advice, Master Walter." The merchant of course expressed his high gratification at the compliment paid him, and promised the King he should always be happy to afford him every assistance in his power, and the audience shortly afterwards broke up.

Master Walter had now obtained nearly the highest point of his ambition, and he easily perceived he should soon obtain the next, and be appointed one of the King's councillors. Still he felt not the slightest pleasure in the fact. As soon as he had left the palace he went on 'Change, and there remained till he saw a merchant who traded largely in timber. Master Walter immediately addressed him, and inquired what quantity of yew timber he had on hand.

"I have at least fifty loads," said the merchant. "In fact, I have nearly all in the market. How much do you want?"

"That entirely depends on the price," said Master Walter. "If the sum you ask is moderate, perhaps I should be tempted to take the whole, but I should like to see it before I went further in the matter."

"Nothing is easier," said the merchant; "it is all at my wharf at Lambeth. You can see it at once if you please. I am sure you will say you never saw a finer lot of yew timber in your life. Shall we go down to the river side and take a boat?"

Master Walter at first raised some objection, saying it was getting late (it was then at least two hour

after noon), and that another day would do as well,
and other excuses, all of which were invented at the
moment, as he did not wish the timber merchant to
think he was anxious about the purchase; but the
latter pressed him so warmly that at last he consented, and they went to the river side and hired a
boat to take them over the water. When they had
arrived at the wharf, Master Walter carefully inspected the yew timber, and found great fault with
it; still he said he might possibly make some use of
it, and he ended by making the merchant an offer
for the entire quantity. The merchant for a long
time demurred, till Master Walter said it was getting
so late that it would be impossible to remove it that
day, and if he could not have it in his possession
before night he would give up the purchase. This
frightened the merchant so much that he immediately accepted Master Walter's terms.

Now Master Walter possessed a wharf and a warehouse at Rotherhithe, and as the tide had just begun
to ebb, and as there were two empty barges lying
alongside the wood merchant's wharf, he immediately
hired them. Having got together some porters, he
put the yew timber in the barges, and then had it
carried down to his own warehouse by the river side.
When the timber was neatly stacked away, he hired
another wherry, and he and the wood merchant
landed at the Tower, and proceeded to Master Walter's
counting-house, where the wood was paid for and the
merchant left him. All being completed, Master

Walter entered his house, when he found that Bertha had gone to spend the evening at the Lord Mayor's private house in Aldgate, with whose family she was on terms of great intimacy. Master Walter then took some refreshment, but his head felt so heavy, that after he had finished he laid himself down on his bed, telling his servant to call him at eight o'clock, and have a litter ready that he might go and fetch his daughter.

When the time arrived he proceeded to the Lord Mayor's house, and pleading indisposition, brought his daughter away, and saw her no more that night.

The next morning Bertha and her father met at breakfast. He received her with great affection, as far as words went, but there was a coldness about his tone which for the moment chilled her. She soon, however, recovered herself, for her curiosity had been greatly excited by what she had heard the evening before. The Lord Mayor had told her that Master Walter had been introduced to the King, who had not only received him with great courtesy and condescension, but had taken him into high favour as well, and there was every probability of his being made one of his Majesty's privy council.

Poor Bertha had not slept that night, so much had she been agitated by the news. Visions of being introduced at court feasts, court balls, and gaieties and festivities of every kind, were running through her brain, as well as other subjects of which perhaps it would be indiscreet to speak.

Bertha opened the conversation by asking her father how he had fared the day before.   "You appeared so ill and tired last night I did not like to trouble you about it."

"Well, my dear, you will be pleased to hear I had the honour of an introduction to his Majesty, who received me very graciously."

"Well, but, father, what did he talk about?"

"That, my dear, of course I am not allowed to tell you."

"Why not?"

"Because it is not usual to entrust state secrets to young ladies, even when they are nineteen years and

a day old.   Besides, frankly, I do not think it would have much interest for you.   This I will tell you.   He asked me what family I had, and I told him one daughter, an awkward countryfied girl, who had seen nothing of society."

"Thank you; and what did the King say?"

"He made no remark, but appeared to think it very possible, when your troublesome bashful friend, the Lord Mayor, spoke and spoilt all."

"What did he say?"

"Oh! you would not like to hear, for I am sure it would shock you."

"I am sure I have nothing to fear," said Bertha, colouring. "What did he say, father?"

"Why, he flatly contradicted me, and said you were a very handsome charming girl, and to his taste there was not your match in the city of London."

"I am very much obliged to him, I am sure," said Bertha. "It is pleasant to know there is some one who can appreciate me. And what did the King say then?"

"That is the most vexatious thing of all, for he seemed to doubt my word, and said he should like to judge for himself; and as he should hold a court on Saturday next, he should request your attendance at it. I am sorry, very sorry, my dear, to give you so much annoyance, but I hope you will bear it with patience. I must trouble you to go after breakfast to Monsieur Joliechose, the French milliner, and order him to make you immediately as splendid a dress to be introduced in as the wit and genius of his country can produce. Let no expense be spared, and do you, my child, to please your old father, look as beautiful as you can."

Bertha hardly knew how to take the words of her father. At any other time she would have accepted them as a piece of good-humoured banter, and from the words themselves there was no reason to think he intended otherwise now, but the whole was uttered in so cold and indifferent a tone she hardly

knew what to think of it. Still the order to go to
the head French milliner of the City, and there
choose the handsomest court dress which could be
made, without any restrictions as to price, was not
an opportunity to be lost, and Bertha in a fit of
extreme obedience rose from the table, and after
kissing her father left him, determining to carry out
his orders forthwith.

As Master Walter was leaving the breakfast room,
one of his clerks entered it, and informed him that
the Master of the Bowyers' Company was at that
moment in the counting-house, and particularly
wished to speak with him. Master Walter immediately went to see his visitor.

"Of what service can I be to you, Master Morgan?"
said the merchant.

"I want to speak to you, Master Walter," said
the Bowyer, "on a subject of great importance. His
Majesty has just sent to us to prepare immediately a
thousand yew bows of the best make, and the whole
of our craft have not sufficient wood to make half
the quantity. Can you advise us on the subject?
There is a report abroad that you are the largest
holder of yew timber. If so, can we not transact
some business together?"

"I shall have much pleasure," said Master Walter;
"but I tell you honestly I will not sell my timber
without receiving an excellent price for it. I very
much suspect, but without being able to give any
reason for it, that the army will be greatly aug-

mented, and then I shall be able to get any price for
my yew timber I may please to ask."

"I admit it to be valuable now; but tell me what
price you ask for it."

Master Walter instantly told him.

"Why," said the Master Bowyer, astonished, "that
is exactly double what you paid for it yesterday."

"How do you know that?"

"From the merchant himself who sold it you. I
went to him yesterday evening, thinking to purchase
the wood of him, and he told me the particulars of
the whole transaction."

"Well," said Master Walter, "I admit it is
true, but I will take no less than the price I ask;
will you give it?"

"I cannot give you an answer," said the Master
Bowyer, "without consulting the livery of our craft.
I will do so to-day, and let you know the result; but
I am afraid they will not give the price you ask."

"Stay," said Master Walter, taking him by the
cloak, "remember the sum I have asked you is only
the price for to-day; I must receive your answer
to-night without fail, or the price I have named
will be doubled to-morrow."

The King again that day sent for Master Walter,
and this time without the Lord Mayor. His Majesty,
as before, seemed highly pleased with his intelligence, and thanked him for the excellent advice he
had given him. Little besides, worthy of record,
occurred that morning; every purchase he made

promised to be lucrative, and everything he sold bore a good profit. In the afternoon he received notice that the corselets had arrived from Milan, and they were immediately transferred from the ship to his warehouses. They seemed when he inspected them to be of a quality much superior to the two or three he had purchased, and he felt certain he should make an immense profit on his bargain. In the course of the afternoon the Master of the Bowyers' Company called on him and told him that his livery had consented to take the yew timber at the price asked, and Master Walter gave him an order on his warehouse-keeper to deliver the wood to the Company.

When he met his daughter at supper, he asked her what success she had had about the dress. She told him that she had found Monsieur Joliechose at home, and that he had shown her many rich and beautiful stuffs, and she had chosen one which she considered would be without equal in the palace. The pattern had only arrived that very day from France, and there was only enough for one dress, so she was certain of what she said. Monsieur Joliechose had promised her on his honour that the dress should be sent home on the Friday evening, and as he was well known to be a man of his word on subjects of importance, she was fully persuaded he would keep his promise.

Master Walter bowed his head in token of approbation, but being evidently in pain he made no remark, and shortly afterwards he went to bed.

Master Walter was now at the height of his good fortune. He was a member of the Privy Council; he was the richest man in London; and everything had turned out exactly as he had wished it. His daughter had been introduced at court, and had been received most graciously. The King, moreover, had told her that a fortnight after the dinner which was to take place at the Guildhall, there would be a grand ball at the palace, at which he commanded that both she and her father should attend.

But in spite of all his success, Master Walter did not appear to be a happy man. Not that he seemed discontented, but he always complained of a weight in his head. Still this did not incapacitate him from business; on the contrary, it was impossible for any individual to be more acute. Of his bodily health he never complained, although it was easy to perceive he became weaker; neither had he the slightest appetite for any food they set before him.

The evening arrived for the feast in the Guildhall. The building was magnificently decorated, and lit up with many thousand torches. All the nobles of the court had been invited, and from the crowded appearance of the tables nearly all must have accepted the invitation. The King was on a raised throne at one end. Nearest to his right hand sat the Lord Mayor, and to his left Master Walter. In a gallery were several ladies of the families of the city magnates who had been permitted to witness the sight, and among them was Bertha. At the sight of her father sitting so near the King, and being spoken to by him so often, her heart beat with pride, yet she was not free from anxiety, so weak and ill did he appear.

But Master Walter's appearance was also noticed by the person who sat at his left hand, and this was no other than Master Ambrose, the King's leech, a man beloved by every one who knew him. He inquired of Master Walter if he did not feel the hall very oppressive from the heat, and Master Walter acknowledged that he did. " I have not been very well lately," he continued, " and I have been thinking of calling on you.for your advice."

" Do so," said the physician, " I will remain at home for you to-morrow morning."

The next day, according to promise, Master Walter called on Master Ambrose. He was introduced into the physician's study, and duly inducted into the patients' chair. Master Ambrose commenced the conversation.

"Now, tell me what is the matter with you; or rather, I think I can tell you."

" What ? " said Master Walter.

" You have lately had something to annoy you, and it has preyed upon your spirits."

" You were never farther from the truth in your life," said Master Walter. "On the contrary, I have not embarked in anything I have not succeeded in."

" You must be a very happy man," said the physician.

" You are in error again. A more miserable wretch does not exist; my life is hateful to me. I receive every blessing, and yet I am not grateful for it. The King honours me extremely, and I care not for it. My daughter loves me affectionately, and I have no affection for her in return, although no man ever had a better daughter."

" But you did not always feel this?" said Master Ambrose.

" Certainly not; it has only been for the last few weeks."

" To what do you attribute it?"

" I am afraid to tell you, lest you should laugh at me."

" You do me injustice," said the physician; " I am incapable of anything of the kind."

" Well then, for what reason I know not, I have lately felt as if my brain were made of glass."

" What can possibly induce you to think that?" said the physician.

" Several reasons. In the first place, my head is so heavy I can hardly support it. In the second, it is exceedingly cold. Thirdly, I see everything clearly before me. I succeed in consequence in everything I attempt, and nobody can deceive me. Lastly, I have lost all sensation of sorrow, excitement, or pleasure. I am no more capable of feeling than a mass of rock crystal."

The physician looked at him carefully for some time. "Master Walter," said he at last, "you must leave London and all business transactions for a week

at least, and then let me see you again."

"But his Majesty will require my attendance."

"I will make your peace with his Majesty," said Master Ambrose, "I shall see him presently. Now go, and think no more of business to-day. You will hear from me to-night. I will write out a course of diet for you to follow."

In the evening the physician not only kept his promise, but enclosed in his letter an order from the Lord Chamberlain to the Governor of Windsor Castle, requesting him to receive Master Walter as the King's guest, to provide him with every amusement, especially the chase—an exercise Master Ambrose strongly recommended to his patient. Next day Bertha and her father left London for Windsor.

# II.

## GILES THE SWINEHERD.

NEARLY three miles to the north of Master Walter de Courcey's town mansion, stood his farm, which not only produced the flour necessary for the consumption of his family and servants, but also cattle, sheep, poultry, and swine. The care of the latter was entrusted to a tall, thin, pale-faced young man of the name of Giles. His cottage was close to the piggeries, and was situated on the extreme corner of the estate. The farm was very extensive, and as the pathways and roads on it were very bad, there was but little communication kept up, especially in winter, between Giles and the bailiff, whose house was on the opposite corner, nearest London. Whenever the bailiff wished to communicate with Giles in the winter season he was in the habit of sending a lad about fifteen years of age with a message, and it was Giles's duty to obey whatever orders the boy brought him.

In the personal character of Giles, who was a bachelor, there was little to admire or respect. He was idle and gluttonous.    Education of course he had none.    In that age gentlemen were rarely able to sign their own names, unless they belonged to the Church, and it was not to be supposed that a swine-herd, living on the extreme verge of a large estate, had had much trouble expended on him.    And grateful indeed was he for his education having been neglected.    As it was, the proper feeding of his swine was a study almost too difficult for him to accomplish ; and it is more than probable, had he not been from time to time encouraged by the bailiff's walking-staff over his shoulders, he never would have arrived at the pitch of perfection he could boast of.    The only study, with the slightest amount of science in it, he took any pleasure in was cooking ; and in this he somewhat excelled, that is to say, if his own tastes were to betaken as the standard of excellence.

The dwelling of Giles was a neat cottage, which he was compelled to keep in good order.    It consisted of one large room, with a communication from the back part to the store-house for the food of his pigs, which again led to the stove for the drying and curing of bacon and hams.    Outside were extensive pig-geries as well as sheds, and a slaughter-house.    All, thanks to the discipline established by the bailiff, were in good order, and any other than so idle and discontented a man as Giles would have considered himself fortunate in possessing so comfortable and convenient an abode.

One fine morning, after a very rainy night, a few weeks from the commencement of our narrative, Giles received a message from the bailiff, ordering him immediately to take two of the finest hams from the store, and carry them as quickly as he could to the house in Bishopsgate Street. When Giles heard this his countenance assumed so terrible an appearance of anger, that the boy did not stop to hear anything he might have to say in reply, but ran back to his master without delay. Giles was perfectly furious, and for some time even mutinous. He first declared he would not go, but a vision of the bailiff's walking-staff induced him reluctantly to alter his determination. He then said, to spite them he would pick out the two hardest and smallest hams he could find. For this purpose, he went into the store-house, and began carefully to examine them, when a singular sum in arithmetic, albeit without his knowing even the meaning of the word, occurred to him. Deduct from two small hard hams the amount of a good flogging (for in those days masters had the right of flogging disobedient servants), and what will be the difference? He calculated this question with a minuteness which did him great credit; and he then resolved that perhaps it would be better to choose two somewhat larger. He went on carefully picking out those he thought would best answer, till at last he ended in selecting the two finest in the store; thus, in fact, fulfilling the order he had received; which he might as well have done at first, and thus saved himself a considerable amount of anxiety and trouble.

He now dressed himself for his march, and having slung the two hams over his shoulders, he started for London. In a short time he again took the trouble of getting out of temper; but there was now some excuse to be urged for him. The roads were heavy with the last night's rain, and the hams certainly

did not weigh less than fifty pounds. Still he kept on his way,—slowly enough, it is true,—and at last arrived in London.

The arrival of Giles at the house in Bishopsgate Street was always the signal for fun among the servants. To tease him appeared to give them pleasure, but as their jokes generally ended by offering him a good dinner, he was accustomed to put up with them good-humouredly enough. This day, however, it was so late when he arrived that dinner was over, and as the cook, not feeling very well, had gone to bed, and the steward, being in an ill-humour, would not allow the door of the larder to be opened, Giles got exceedingly angry at their jesting, and made use of some language it is not necessary to repeat. The men took this in high dudgeon, and a violent quarrel seemed likely to ensue, when Joan, one of the waiting-maids (who, it was suspected, would not have objected to assist Giles in keeping his cottage in order, with the rights and title of wife), came in and acted as peacemaker. She attempted, but in vain, to make Giles understand that all that was said and done by the others was simply in joke. Giles could not see it in that light, and Joan, to facilitate matters, took him from the room, telling him she had something very beautiful to show him, and as the family were now all away, it would be an excellent opportunity for him to see it.

Giles sullenly left the kitchen, and went with her upstairs. She took him into the chamber in which was the Venetian mirror, and showed him his own face in it. He was, for the moment, somewhat surprised, but it gave him no pleasure whatever. Joan, on the contrary, admired her own face in it with every symptom of delight, although she had  performed the same experiment on it fifty times already.

" Is it not beautiful?" she asked her companion.

" Pretty well for that, but I don't see much good in it."

" Why, you can see your face whenever you want."

" And what's the use of that? I know pretty well what I am like already."

" But still it's very beautiful. Do you think you could get the fairies to bring me such a one some night? I wish you'd ask them to do it for me. I am sure in that out-of-the-way cottage of yours you must see plenty of them. It's just the sort of place they would like to live about."

" I only know that if there are any fairies there, or hobgoblins either, I wish they would make themselves a little more useful than they do."

" Why, what would you wish them to do?" said Joan, in a playful manner—"bring you a wife?"

" Not exactly."

" What then?"

" Well, I wish they'd do all my work for me, and bring me plenty to eat; that's all I want of them."

Joan, in a fit of disgust, left her unsympathetic companion, who followed her downstairs. He tried again to get into conversation with her, but it was quite useless, she would have nothing to say to him. He then essayed to speak to the other servants, but with no better success; and at last, finding himself avoided by all, he took up his cap and staff and left the house.

He was in an intensely bad humour when he left

London and bent his steps homewards. When he arrived near his cottage it was dark night; and he was so tired he could hardly drag one foot after the other. He was also faint and hungry, and he cursed his ill-fortune that he should have to light a fire and cook his evening meal before he could eat it, and when he had finished it that he should have to feed his swine before he could go to bed. When he came in sight of his cottage, he was greatly astonished to find it lit up, and a good fire evidently

burning on the hearth. He recovered himself, however, and walked rapidly forward, so great was the effect his curiosity had on him. At last he arrived, and on opening his door he was not a little surprised to find two large wax candles stuck in wooden candlesticks on the table, and a magnificent log fire burning in the fire-place. But what astonished him more than all was to see standing on the table a little man dressed with exquisite neatness. He could not have been a foot high, yet he was so beautifully formed that it would have been impossible to find a more perfect model. His dress consisted of a tight pair of white silk pantaloons with stripes running down them, and a neat-made velvet jacket tight to his body. His clothes fitted him so beautifully, he might have been born in them. On his head he wore a neat velvet cap with a white feather in it, a natty-looking little dagger, about the size of a pen-knife, hung by his side, and a little silver whistle was slung round his neck by a silken thread.

As soon as Giles had somewhat recovered from his surprise, the figure, with an air of the most exquisite puppyism, took off his cap and stood bareheaded. He waited a short time, as if expecting to be spoken to, but as Giles said nothing he took the initiative:

"Welcome home, my lord; we have been expecting you for some time, and at last we became somewhat alarmed, fearing you might have lost yourself in the darkness of the night."

"And pray who may you be?" said Giles.

"My name, my lord, is Capsicum. His Majesty Oberon, the king of the fairies, hearing it was your

wish that his people should do your work for you and
find you in food, ordered me to bring a party of fairies
to your house to attend on your wishes, and to carry
them out to the best of their abilities. He also bade
me take with me a troop of goblins to do the out-door
and grosser work. I am afraid, from the short notice
I had, you will hardly find things in the order I
could wish them to be; but to-morrow I hope everything will be done to your perfect satisfaction. Is
there any order you would kindly favour me with at
present?"

"I most sincerely wish," said Giles, "you would
go directly and get me something to eat, for I am
starving."

"I will immediately order in the butler to obey
your commands. My position in your lordship's
establishment is that of major-domo."

So saying, he placed his silver whistle to his

lips, and instantly another fairy entered the room.

Although in size the new comer was no taller than
Capsicum, there was a marked difference in their
appearance. Vineleaf, the butler, was a stout, respectable, grave-looking fairy, whose countenance bore
such an intense expression of respect, that it appeared
doubtful if he were really capable of smiling.   Capsicum told him it was his lordship's wish that dinner
should be on the table forthwith; and Vineleaf, bowing low, immediately left the room. As soon as he had

gone, Capsicum explained that Vineleaf was to act as
butler.   He said he thoroughly understood his duties;

in fact, he had but one fault. He was occasionally too
fond of tasting the wine he had under his care. He,
Capsicum, had however given him especial instructions to be on his best behaviour, or he should be
under the painful necessity of reporting him at head-
quarters. Capsicum had hardly finished his remark,
when at least twenty male fairies entered the room.
Many of them, in pairs, bore dishes which would have
been too heavy for them single-handed, although they
contained portions of cooked food which ordinary
mortals would have considered ridiculously small, and
others carried lighter viands and fruit: one an apple;
another, although it was winter, a peach; a third, a
bunch of dried grapes. All carried something, and
the whole made up a dinner far more copious than
the heartiest man would have been able to eat at one
meal. All were dressed in a neat uniform livery,
and, in spite of their diminutive size, made really a
very grand appearance. As it was naturally impossible for them to reach to the table, the genius of
Capsicum had improvised a sort of staircase out of
different articles he had found in the house, and by
its help the fairies mounted on the table, and placed
the dishes in their proper order. When all was arranged, Vineleaf informed Giles that his dinner was
ready. His chair was then pushed nearer the table,
and he commenced his meal.

At first he was somewhat disgusted at the small
portions placed before him, but as each was consumed
another supplied its place; and at last he became

content with the arrangement. The dishes were all
exquisitely cooked, and of the most delicate description; and the service was admirably managed, although the plan followed was somewhat singular.
As the diminutive size of the servants precluded the
possibility of their standing on the floor, they placed
themselves on the table; yet so much order was observed, that not the slightest inconvenience occurred
among them. Vineleaf had placed himself at the
right hand of Giles, and from time to time filled his
horn with the most delicious wine. As Giles drank,
his spirits rose, and in a short time he had become
fully accustomed to the scene before him, and felt every
inch a lord. From time to time, however, unpleasant ideas entered his mind. He remembered, in
the first place, that his hogs had not been fed, and an
unpleasant vision of the bailiff's staff presented itself
before him; but still he had philosophy enough to
determine to enjoy his dinner while he was about it.

The quantity he consumed was perfectly wonderful.

He was naturally a
glutton, and on the
present occasion he
showed that qualifi-
cation in a perfectly
developed manner.
Capsicum, who also
stood on the table,
seemed perfectly de-
lighted with his lord's appetite, and as he attacked

each successive dish placed before him, his satisfaction appeared to increase in proportion. But everything must have an end, and there was one to Giles's appetite. At last he pushed his chair from the table, and placed it by the fire. In his long, lank figure there were evident symptoms that he had done justice to his meal; and he now determined to enjoy his ease at his own fireside. The servants rapidly debarrassed the table of the rest of the feast, and in a short time Giles was left alone with Capsicum, who had now

placed himself beside the fire, and in front of his master.

"I hope the dinner was to your lordship's satisfaction," he remarked.

"Yes, pretty well for that," answered Giles, determined to appear as if he had been used to repasts of the kind.

" I hope," said Capsicum, " that if your lordship noticed any little irregularity you will kindly excuse it. I trust to-morrow things will be done in better style."

Giles graciously bowed his head.

" Do the liveries meet with your lordship's approbation ? If not, they shall be altered. It was only about six hours ago that I received his Majesty's commands to wait on you, and I have been rather hurried, or I would have paid greater attention to the servants' dress."

" I remarked nothing to complain of," said Giles, with great dignity.

" It gives me much satisfaction to hear your lordship say so. Would your lordship wish to see the female servants to-night, or will you put it off till the morning ? They are all ready to appear should you desire it. I flatter myself you will be pleased with them. I assure you I chose such to attend you as I thought you would like."

" Yes," said Giles, " I have no objection to their coming in now."

Capsicum blew his silver whistle and a footman entered.

" Tell the female servants to wait on his lordship," he said.

The footman disappeared, and the next moment a long file of female fairies, each more beautiful than tho other, with the exertion of the housekeeper, who was somewhat too stout for perfect symmetry, entered the room. They were neatly dressed in white, their costume being perfectly uniform. They strongly resembled, in miniature, those we are accustomed to see on the stage at the opera, with the exception that their faces were not painted, and they were without those absurd spangled verdigris-coloured wings which theatrical managers from time immemorial appear to think have been worn in Fairyland, utterly ignoring the impossibility of their wearing cashmere shawls (always a weakness with fairies) along with those appendages. As they walked before Giles, Capsicum mentioned their names, and  explained their various duties. As each passed, she

gracefully curtsied, and then disappeared through

the door. When they had all left, Capsicum remarked, with the most perfect foppishness of manner, that he trusted his lordship was pleased with them, as he flattered himself he had a keen eye for female beauty; to which Giles graciously remarked that they met with his most perfect approbation.

A silence of some minutes now ensued, during which the mind of Giles was occupied on a most unpleasant subject. The pigs had not been fed, and he knew perfectly well that it must be done before he went to bed, especially as there were several litters of young pigs, whose mothers might suffer severely from any neglect on his part. Still he hardly knew in what way it was to be done, for it was impossible to mention a subject of the kind to the exquisite little dandy that stood before him, and he knew that if he went out without speaking on the subject he would be watched, which would be equally derogatory. The silence, however, was broken by the loquacious Capsicum :

" Would not your lordship like to have your boots taken off ? "

" Yes—No—Well, perhaps you may as well do it," was the reply.

" Pardon me, your lordship," said Capsicum, with great respect, but at the same time showing that his feelings had been hurt by the request, " but that does not come within a fairy's duties. I will send for the captain of the goblins, who will attend you immediately."

So saying he blew his silver whistle, and when the footman appeared said, " Send that fellow Calfskin here."

The footman bowed and retired, and a minute afterwards he returned with the captain of the goblins.

It would be difficult to imagine two creatures bearing any resemblance to the human race who differed more in form and ex-  pression of countenance than Capsicum and Calfskin. The one was slim, graceful, and rapid in his movements; the other was strong, heavy, and slow. Capsicum, with all his foppery and self-conceit, had an immense amount of intellect in his handsome countenance; while Calfskin showed scarcely more ability than a brute. His brow was low though broad, his face flat and square, and his lower jaw heavy. In height he was taller by two or three inches than Capsicum, but so wide across the shoulders and squat in form, that he scarcely looked so tall. To sum up all, Capsicum seemed the incarnation of gracefulness and intelligence, while Calfskin was that of heavy brute force.

As soon as Calfskin had made his obeisance, Capsicum said to him, " Fellow, his lordship wishes his boots taken off. Be careful that you do it without hurting him, or we shall quarrel. We must have no clumsiness here."

Calfskin respectfully bowed, and with more skill  than he would have been thought capable of, succeeded in taking off Giles's boots. He was then on the point of retiring, when Capsicum addressed him with great sternness :

" Have you no report, fellow, to give of the manner in which the duties of your charge have been performed ? You will certainly get yourself severely punished if I find any more of this remissness on your part."

" I beg your lordship's pardon," said Calfskin, bowing very low. " The pigs have all been fed, and their beds have been made up for the night. I am also happy to say that the young litters are doing well ; not a casualty of any kind has occurred."

" That will do," said Capsicum ; " if his lordship has no other question to ask, you may depart."

Giles merely made a negative gesture, yawning the while, and Calfskin left the room with the boots. As soon as he was gone Capsicum said, " I see your lordship is fatigued, and probably would wish to retire for the night. If you have no commissions for me, I will respectfully take my leave."

Giles said he wanted nothing more, and Capsicum left him.

When Giles awoke the next morning, he found the room had been dusted and put in order, his boots were by the side of his bed, and a glorious fire was burning on the hearth; yet all this had been done so silently, that he had not been aware of the presence of any one in his room. He arose and leisurely dressed himself. When his toilet was fully completed, he seated himself in his chair, which had been placed ready for him by the fire, and was on the point of calling Capsicum, when he found that ubiquitous gentleman standing before him, cap in hand, waiting for his lordship to speak.

Giles seemed to wish to say something worthy of a lord, and in fact was turning over in his mind some polite method of addressing his major-domo, but it all ended in simply, " Bring me my breakfast."

The silver whistle was immediately put into requisition, and a dozen servants, who had anticipated the order, entered with the breakfast, and placed it on the table in the same manner and with the same regularity as the dinner had been served the evening before. Of tea and coffee there was none, but warm sweet wines deliciously spiced supplied their place. There were eggs cooked in every mode, beautiful white and brown bread, broiled ham and cakes, and in fact everything that could tempt the appetite. Giles ate of everything, and it was only when he could eat no more that he left off.

As soon as breakfast was over, Capsicum invited him to see the arrangements he had made in the house for the servants, as well as for carrying on the routine out of doors. Giles, who by the bye was not particularly disposed to move, rose from his chair and followed his major-domo. They went into the kitchen, and there the housekeeper, in a new cap, joined them, and from time to time entered into the conversation, at least as long as they remained inside the house. This seemed particularly to annoy Capsicum, who wished it to appear that he was lord and master of all the domestic establishment. The kitchen was certainly a miracle of fairy ingenuity and neatness. Capsicum had placed it in the storeroom in which the pigs' victuals were kept, but in that part nearest to the sitting-room; and it was carefully shut off from the rest of the storehouse by twigs gracefully plaited together, and so closely and neatly that it was impossible to perceive a fissure in any part of it. To any one but a phlegmatic individual like Giles, the inspection of the arrangements of the kitchen would have afforded a rich treat. Fifty little furnaces, each not capable of holding so much fuel as would go into a tea-cup, were ranged along the wall, and on wooden shelves were placed innumerable little saucepans of a size corresponding with the furnaces,

all of copper and beautifully bright. The honours of
the kitchen were performed by a stout middle-aged

male fairy dressed in white, with a white cap on his
head and a knife stuck in his girdle. He went
through the task with a grace like that of Soyer or
Francatelli, when explaining to visitors the magnificent kitchen of the Reform Club. During the
whole time a double row of under-cooks and fairy
kitchen-maids in neat uniform dresses stood silently
by, apparently deeply impressed with the dignity
of the visitor.

On leaving the kitchen Capsicum showed Giles the
sleeping accommodation for the male servants; and
then taking him into the stoves used for drying the
bacon and hams, he was on the point of showing
him the sleeping apartments of the female servants,
when the fairy housekeeper interposed and requested
his lordship's patience, as that apartment was hardly
ready for his inspection. At her interference Capsi-

cum appeared highly offended, and whispered to Giles as they left the house that she was an ill-tempered frumpish old thing, and he much regretted having chosen her to wait upon his lordship.

Giles now inspected the out-door arrangements, attended by Capsicum and Calfskin, who had been summoned for the purpose. They first cast a glance into the quarters of the goblins, but Giles cared little for their comfort, and Capsicum wore on his face the while an expression of supreme disgust. They then visited the piggeries, and here Giles for the first time seemed really pleased with the efficiency displayed. The pigs had not only been fed, but an entire army of goblins were employed in cleaning out the sties. Everything was in perfect order, and there was not a single thing of which Giles could complain, or he would have conscientiously done so.

He now strolled leisurely round the house, conversing with Capsicum. Meantime there was something pressing anxiously on his mind. It was, that if the bailiff should make him a visit and find how comfortable he had been made, he might order him to some other part of the farm, where his position would not be a jot more agreeable than it was the morning before. Capsicum appeared intuitively to understand his master's thoughts.

"It is my duty," said he, "to inform your lordship that all the arrangements which have been made are solely for your own use. Nothing would

annoy his Majesty our king more than that it
should be thought his people were servants to mortals, for whom in general he entertains a supreme
dislike. Whenever a messenger comes from London,
or the bailiff pays you a visit, everything we have
done will be invisible. Not a fairy or goblin will be
seen, and he may walk all over the place without
finding anything different from its ordinary condition. I must therefore trust to your discretion that
you will say nothing about it."

Giles readily made the promise, as nothing could
possibly have better suited his views.

For some time Giles's life appeared to him one of
perfect happiness. His gluttonous propensities were
pampered to the utmost, and he had positively
nothing to do. So skilful were all Capsicum's
arrangements, and so effectually were they carried
out, that not a feature of the supernatural was
visible to general observers. A message came one
afternoon from the bailiff to send two flitches of
bacon to his house the next morning, and Giles
was somewhat puzzled how to execute the order
without lowering his dignity in the eyes of the
fairies. He passed a very troubled night in thinking
on the subject, and rose the next morning without having come to any conclusion. He determined, however, that he would breakfast first, and
then take the question into serious consideration.
Capsicum as usual made his appearance at the
breakfast table, and in course of conversation in-

formed him that the order had already been executed. Calfskin, about midnight, had pressed all hands,

and the goblins had carried two flitches of bacon-to the bailiff's, and had deposited them in his house before any of the family were stirring.

A few days afterwards the bailiff paid a visit of inspection to the piggeries, and was much pleased at the excellent order they were in. Capsicum had seen him approach, and all the fairies and goblins with their separate arrangements were immediately ordered to be invisible. He saw only one thing that surprised him, and that was the great improvement which had taken place in Giles's appearance. He was considerably stouter, so much so in fact that the bailiff, had he met him elsewhere, would hardly have known him.

But although at the commencement everything appeared *couleur de rose* to Giles, he found in the end that the possession of a large number of servants brought with it its anxieties as well as its pleasures. He was considerably annoyed on more than one occasion at the squabbles which took place among them, particularly the female fairies. They were as susceptible, in fact, to love and jealousy as mere mortals. Capsicum was the Adonis of the party, and he flirted with them all. This, however, did not exactly meet their views, and each in her turn attempted to captivate him for her own especial slave. If he showed more attention to one than the others considered proper, the neglected ones were most indignant. To improve somewhat this state of things, he paid attentions to two at the same time, and the result was a most disgraceful scene of cap-pulling.

Giles himself fell somewhat into these intrigues. A very beautiful fairy, of the name of Rosebud, considering that Capsicum did not pay sufficient homage to her charms, set her cap at his master. It must not be supposed she had the slightest affection for Giles. The attention she showed him was solely to arouse the jealousy, and probably the love, of Capsicum. With feminine tact she watched for an opportunity of making an attack on Giles's heart. One occurred at last, and she profited by it. He had contrived to catch a severe cold, and she took upon herself the task of nursing him. Her manner at first was merely respectful, but by degrees, when she saw that he was pleased, she became more familiar. At last a regular flirtation was established between them; but to do her justice it was principally when Capsicum was present that she took the greatest liberties. She would then stand on the table when Giles took his gruel and feed him with a spoon, and

occasionally, if he spilt any on his dress, she would tap him playfully on the nose with it, while Capsicum stood by with folded arms and a sneer on his countenance, the very model of a fairy Mephistopheles.

But Giles had reason to be somewhat discontented with the improper conduct of the fairies generally. One clear moonlight night they all met to dance under an old oak tree in front of his cottage, and their behaviour on this occasion gave him great annoyance. The ball was by no means regulated according to his ideas of propriety; indeed a modern casino was, in point of proper demeanour, a court ball in comparison.

Another subject in course of time began to give

Giles some uneasiness. It has already been stated that he had become stouter, and that the bailiff had noticed it. He was now inclined to be absolutely corpulent. His clothes fitted him so tightly that they hindered considerably the few movements he made, and a company of fairy tailors had to be sent for to enlarge them. This was done to the extreme limits of the cloth, and for a few days Giles experienced some relief; but he increased in size so rapidly that he was again obliged to have recourse to some expedient by which he might obtain ease. There was but one, and that was to have a new suit of clothes made for him. This was accordingly done, ample room being allowed for growing. Still he went on increasing in fat, till at last he became fairly alarmed.

He now determined to be more moderate in his diet, and to take only four meals a day instead of six. But he found it impossible to carry out his good resolutions. No sooner had he formed them than the viands, tempting as they had been before, were now so exquisitely cooked and so delicious, that he found the attempt to abstain from them an utter impossibility. It was no longer simply at his meals that he ate. There was now always something appetising placed before him, and he could not resist it, although he felt that after each snack he took his weight of fat was greater than before.

One morning a certain virtuous resolution presented itself to his imagination. It struck him that if he worked a little instead of being idle all day, it might do him good. Resolving to try the experiment, he ordered Capsicum to tell the captain of the goblins not to clean out the piggeries that morning.

"May I be so bold as to inquire the reason?" said Capsicum.

"I think a little exercise might do me good, and I will clean them out myself."

"Pardon me, your lordship, but it is impossible."

"How impossible?"

"It would be breaking faith with the king my master," said Capsicum. "You wished to have plenty to eat and nothing to do, and he has obliged you in both things. You, in your turn, must keep your part of the bargain."

"I don't care one straw about the king your master," said Giles. "I am not going to be governed by him, I can tell you. It's my pleasure to work this morning, and I will do it."

"Take care, my lord," said Capsicum; "his Majesty is not a potentate to be disobeyed with impunity."

"We'll see that," said Giles, and he immediately went out of doors.

He had, however, hardly looked around him when he perceived six enormous, savage-looking bears prowling round the house.

"Where did these come from?" said Giles, in a terrified voice.

"I cannot exactly say," replied Capsicum, "but they are evidently sent by the king my master, and will certainly tear you in pieces if you do not return."

Giles, without saying a word, re-entered the house, and found on the table a dish of lobsters so exquisitely prepared that he was not proof against the temptation, and he soon swallowed the whole.

His fat continued to increase, and one fine morning he determined to leave the cottage, if only to take a little exercise; but he had so much difficulty in getting through the door that the thought struck him if he should at all grow in size when he was out he would not be able to get in again, and that he should become an easy prey to the bears if they were still in the neighbourhood. So he gave up the attempt. He now resigned himself to his fate, and increased so much in rotundity that his life became a perfect burden to him, and he sighed again to be the lank figure he was before he made the acquaintance of the fairies.

# III.

## THE MERCER'S APPRENTICE.

In a pleasant country lane leading from Bethnal Green to Houndsditch lived a very poor but very respectable widow, Dame Matears. Her means of existence were derived from a very slender pension from the Clothworkers' Company, of which her husband had been a freeman, and from the trifle which, being a good needlewoman, she earned in making coifs for Master Longhose, a mercer in Chepe, to whom her son Luke was apprenticed. Luke Matears was now nearly out of his time, being within a few months of twenty-one years of age. He was exceedingly handsome, tall, and well-proportioned, and all who saw him said it was a pity so fine a young man should be obliged to pass his life in selling tapes and laces in a mercer's shop. But Luke had other qualifications; he was an excellent son, and his widowed mother perfectly doated on him. He resided with her, but he left the house early in the morning, and seldom returned to it till it was late at night. The road which he was accustomed to take led him past the mansion of Master Walter de Courcey; and one afternoon as he was coming home he noticed a great crowd gathered round the entrance to see a foreign nobleman alight from his litter. The circumstance interested him the more as the nobleman was so ill and weak he had to be carried in the arms of men from the litter into the house. Luke told his mother of it, who replied that she had heard in the morning that a very wealthy Venetian nobleman was expected to arrive there that night. She was acquainted with the housekeeper at Master Walter's, who occasionally used to give her little commissions to execute. That day she had taken home a coif she had been entrusted to alter, and the house-keeper had shown her the fittings-up of the chamber the foreigner was to sleep in, which were of a most gorgeous description.

"It's a fine thing, Luke, to be a rich city merchant. I hope some day to see you one."

"Nonsense, mother; how can a poor fellow like me ever expect to be anything of the kind? If I can only get bread and cheese I ought to be contented."

"Still, my dear, with industry and perseverance, you may do a great deal. There have been many merchants who began life as poor as you are, and ended by being Lord Mayor."

"It was not by selling tapes and laces they did it though, mother dear."

"Never mind, do you continue honest and industri-ous, and more unlikely things than that may happen."

For some weeks no further conversation was held on the subject of the foreigner; but Luke one evening brought home the intelligence that the Venetian nobleman was dead, and that Master Walter had inherited from him a beautiful glass mirror which was the wonder of the whole city. It was as white as silver, but so clear that it appeared to a person looking in it as if there was an image of himself at a short distance before him, so perfect in every respect that he might almost fancy he could touch it. Luke concluded by remarking how much he should like to see it.

"Why do you not ask permission?" said his mother.

"Because, in the first place, I know no one employed at Master Walter's; and in the second, I understand so many people have applied to see it, that the servants have injunctions to show it to no one without an especial order from the merchant himself, and he has just gone into the country for change of air, in consequence of suffering from severe pains in the head."

"Never mind, Luke," said Dame Matears, "I will get you a sight of it if you wish it. I am sure the housekeeper will not object to show it to me, and you can accompany me at the time, and she will be too good-natured to refuse you; that I know well enough."

Luke was not a little pleased when he heard of the influential acquaintance his mother had in the rich man's house, and he begged she would call on the housekeeper on the morrow, when he would go with her. He then appointed to meet his mother opposite the church of St. Botolph the next afternoon, as he was sure he should be sent near it on a commission by his master about that time. All things being properly settled between them, they went to bed.

The next afternoon Luke met his mother as arranged, and they called at Master Walter de Courcey's house. Dame Matears took with her the pattern of a new coif lately arrived from France, which had been lent her by a milliner she worked for, and the shape of the coif and civility of the poor woman so won the heart of the influential housekeeper that she asked her if she would like to see the wonderful mirror which had lately arrived from Venice. Dame Matears replied that it was the greatest wish of her heart; but she hoped the housekeeper would not be offended if she asked permission for her son, who was waiting in the court-yard, to accompany them. The housekeeper, after a proper amount of demur, fearing the discretion of so young a man (as their visit was to be a perfect secret), consented. It should be stated, however, that before giving her answer she had glanced through the open window into the court yard, and there saw one of the handsomest, most modest-looking young men she had ever set eyes on, and it was this which principally induced her to allow him to accompany his mother.

The housekeeper conducted them up-stairs, and taking a key from a bunch which hung by her side, she opened the door of the room containing the magic mirror. Both mother and son were struck with its wonderful beauty, and were silent for some moments as if they were standing before a holy relic. Presently they regained the use

of their tongues; and they made full use of them, especially the mother. " Nothing was ever so beautiful." " It must have been made by the hands of the angels; mortals could never have succeeded in making anything of the sort ;" and many more expressions of the same kind fell from their lips with remarkable fluency. Luke asked what might be the meaning of the strange-looking characters round the top of the glass ; but on this point the housekeeper could give him no information. She said she believed that as it was made in foreign parts, where the letters were not the same as in England, it was simply the name of the manufacturer. Of course, Dame Matears admitted that nothing was more likely; and she began to examine, and possibly to admire, her own reflection in the glass. What pleased her immeasurably more, however, was that of her son.

" You can now see, Luke," she said, laughing, "what an ugly fellow you are. Don't you think so, madam?" addressing the housekeeper.

" Well," said that influential person, laughing also, " I will not say that. If he is as good as he's good-looking, he'll pass muster in a crowd."

"I have no right to complain of him on that score," said Dame Matears. "I will acknowledge no woman in London has a better or more affectionate son."

"There's some good about him then," said the housekeeper; " I always like a son that's kind to his mother."

" Come here," said Dame Matears to him, " and look at yourself well in the glass, and tell me what you think of yourself."

"I think, mother," said he, laughing, "that if I were as well dressed as that nobleman we saw entering Crosby Palace just now, I should look far better than he did."

"I think you would," said his mother; " and I should like to see you well dressed in a magnificent suit of velvet."

" I sincerely wish the same thing, mother; I should like to wear a dress of that kind every day. But I may as well wish at the same time that I had a purse of gold always in my pouch. Without that, such clothes would be of little use."

" But, Luke," said Dame Matears, " before you are likely to obtain anything of the kind you must grow a little older; you cannot expect to be rich at your age."

" I would not object to that," said Luke.

" You must get a beard first," said the house-keeper, glancing at the young fellow's smooth chin.

" I should like very much to have a beard," said Luke colouring, and looking at his face in the mirror ; " but I suppose it will come in time."

The mother and son remained conversing a short time longer, and then, thanking the housekeeper for her kindness, they left.

Next morning Dame Matears tapped as usual at her son's chamber door, to inform him it was time to rise and go to business, and she then busied her-self in preparing his breakfast.

Luke first stretched himself, and felt very much as if he should like  to sleep a little longer; but as his master was severe on the point of punctual attend-ance, he made an effort, and leaped from his bed half asleep. He was on the point of commencing his morning ablu-tions, and had already placed the towel to his face, when his hands dropped by his side, and he remained for some time in a state of perfect astonishment. He almost doubted if he were not still asleep. He reflected a moment, and then came to the conclusion that he was fully awake, and yet his chin, which the night before was as smooth as a young girl's, was now covered with a handsome beard. In his surprise he hurried to put on some necessary article of dress, and then to call his mother to notice his altered appearance; but his astonishment was still more increased by finding that his clothes had been removed, and in their place was a magnificent dress of dark purple velvet, an exquisitely chiselled silver-hilted dagger, a superb pouch richly embroidered in gold, and a rich cap to match.

After a few minutes' hesitation he dressed himself in the suit before him, and when his toilette was fully completed, he descended to his mother.

Dame Matears, who was busy with the breakfast, did not hear him descend; and when she did see him, her surprise, as might naturally be expected, so overcame her that she was incapable of speaking. In fact she did not recognise him, but imagined it was some rich nobleman who had casually dropped in to ask his way, and she made him a profound curtsey.

" Do you not know me, mother ? " said Luke, somewhat alarmed, for he had imagined the rich dress he had on was in some way connected with her, forgetting at the moment the fact of his having a beard.

Dame Matears almost fainted when she found the magnificently dressed young nobleman was her own son.

"Luke, my dear," she said, "take off those things, for there is certainly witchcraft in them."

"Witchcraft or no, mother, I shall wear them if there is no other person to claim them. How do you think I look in them?"

"Beautifully; but I don't like them. I am all in a tremble; do, my dear, go and take them off."

But Luke was obstinate, and insisted on wearing them, and by degrees his mother became so infatuated with his appearance that she made no further remonstrance, and both mother and son began examining the different points of the dress. Presently they came to the pouch, the gold embroidery of which pleased the old needlewoman immensely.

" Let us see what the inside is like," said Luke, and he plunged his hand into it. The next moment he withdrew it, holding in it a heavy purse of gold. He emptied the contents on the table, and the eyes of both mother and son glistened as they beheld the glittering coins.

" Mother," said Luke, " do you remember our wish yesterday? This is certainly a gift from the fairies, and I know no reason why I should not accept it. We have now enough to make us both rich for life. Take you those," he said, pushing over to her five or six coins; "I shall try my fortune with the remainder." So saying he replaced the money in his purse, and Dame Matears, without further objection, took up the others.

They now sat down to their breakfast, but neither had any appetite.

" I suppose, Luke," said his mother, " you will not go to business to-day; shall I go and tell your master ? "

" Mother, I have no master," said Luke, with great dignity, not unmixed with anger; " pray never mention that word before me again."

" What then do you propose doing, dear ? "

" I shall remain quietly here till noon, and then perhaps I shall stroll down to Paul's if the weather keeps fine."

Mother and son sat together some time longer,

she feasting her eyes on her son's beauty, and he considering what steps he should take so as to be able to mix with the higher classes without suspicion. Little conversation passed between them. To the few remarks she made he returned short and petulant answers, and it was easy to perceive that already his new-fledged dignity had a most prejudicial effect on his disposition. When it was near noon he took up his cap, and without even saying adieu to his mother, left the house.

He was somewhat nervous at first starting, lest he should be recognised by any of his acquaintances. Not only, however, did his clothes disguise him perfectly, but his beard added at least six or seven years to his age. As he walked along he soon began to acquire confidence, and he was greatly flattered by the audible remarks of the passers-by on the magnificence and beauty of his appearance. He passed boldly before his master's shop in Chepe, and was greatly amused at seeing his fellow-apprentices rush forward to look at the splendidly dressed stranger. For a moment he thought of entering it and purchasing something, but prudence kept him back, lest he might by chance be discovered.

At last he arrived at Paul's, and without hesitation he mixed with the crowd of well-dressed persons he met there. The weather was fine, and many of the nobility were there, but not one among them was dressed with so much magnificence or in so good taste as himself. It was some time before he entered into conversation with any one, but at last he took the opportunity of speaking to a splendidly dressed young man, evidently of noble family, who answered him most courteously. In a very short time he found his new acquaintance was the eldest son of the Baron of Winterbourne, a wealthy nobleman of great notoriety, but suspected of being but little attached to the king.

Luke on his part was obliged to introduce himself to his new found friend. He had already concocted a tale, and he told it with unblushing effrontery, for with his new position he had acquired the facility of a hardened liar.

He described himself as Sir Kenneth Gordon, from Scotland, where he had large estates. He had come to England principally for the purpose of seeing London, but as the roads were bad he had ridden on in advance of his retainers, who he expected would arrive the next day. As it was, he found himself in considerable difficulty. He did not know a person in London, nor did he know the name of a good hostelry. Could Sir Hubert inform him of one ?

"Nothing can be easier," Sir Hubert replied. "I shall have much pleasure in conducting you immediately to one pleasantly situated in Southwark."

As they left Paul's, Sir Hubert asked him if he had not a horse.

Luke replied that he had not. His own had broken down about a mile before arriving in London, and he should be obliged to buy one the next day. Sir Hubert kindly promised on the morrow to accompany him to a dealer, and the pair then started off for the " Tabard," in Southwark.

On their road Sir Hubert pointed out to his companion the various objects of interest they passed, and Luke, on his part, simulated admirably his surprise at objects he had been acquainted with since he had been a child. London Bridge, which he had crossed a thousand times, particularly excited his wonder, and he gazed with the greatest interest at the shipping he saw in the river. They continued their course till they had arrived at the "Tabard," when Sir Hubert introduced Luke to the host as his especial friend, and requested that every attention might be shown to him. A couple of rooms were immediately placed at his disposal, and Sir Hubert left him, promising to call again in the evening. Luke then ordered his dinner, and afterwards amused himself by strolling about the park in Bermondsey and the Bishop's Gardens, till evening approached, when he returned to the inn to wait the arrival of his new acquaintance.

Sir Hubert was not only true to his appointment, but he brought with him two friends, evidently young men of condition, but certainly of very dissipated habits, judging at least from their conversation. This by no means displeased Luke, who began to consider language of this kind as characteristic of high breeding, and he imitated it to the best of his power. Wine was called for, and shortly afterwards one of Sir

Hubert's friends proposed a game at dice. These were instantly sent for, and the whole party were soon engaged in play. Luke drank freely and played deeply—and lost. He continued until he had not a single gold piece left, when his friends shortly afterwards bade him farewell, and left him thoroughly intoxicated.

The next morning the remembrance of the last night's debauch came painfully before him, accompanied by a violent headache. He arose ill and dispirited : what to do he knew not. He remembered perfectly well that he had lost the whole of his money, and what excuse to make to his host puzzled him extremely. However, he dressed himself, and on taking up his pouch was somewhat surprised at its weight. He placed his hand in it, and drew out his purse as full of gold as it was the morning before. His fear and anxiety immediately vanished, and with a radiant air, in spite of his headache, he entered the sitting room.

He now breakfasted sumptuously, and afterwards sent for the host, and asked in what amount he was indebted to him. The innkeeper, however, requested he would not trouble himself about such a trifle, and assured him that when he left the inn it would be quite time enough to settle his account. This mark of confidence greatly pleased Luke, and he sat down to wait for the arrival of Sir Hubert, who had promised to call on him at an early hour. Sir Hubert kept him waiting but a short time, and

after the first civilities were over, they left the house
together, and bent their steps towards the City.
On their road Luke
confided to his com-
panion that he was
much distressed at
the non-appearance
of his servants, the
more so as he was
positively destitute of
all clothing except
"those poor things"
upon him, as he
called them; and he
asked Sir Hubert if

he could recommend him to a merchant where he
could get what he wanted, of good quality, for price
was a matter of indifference. Sir Hubert told him
he would take him to the most honest tradesman in
London, where he would be able to obtain anything
he wanted.

The pair now walked leisurely along, conversing
together in a very friendly manner, and attracting, by
the magnificence of their apparel, the notice of all
the passers by, till they arrived at Chepe, when, to
Luke's intense horror, Sir Hubert led him straight to
the shop of Master Longhose. When Luke entered
it he blushed so deeply he was obliged to keep his
back to the light to prevent its being noticed by his
companion. In a short time, however, finding he

was not discovered, he regained possession of his presence of mind; and as he had frequently seen

young noblemen in the shop, he contrived to imitate them in a very clever manner. He was imperious and insolent, and gave his orders to Master Longhose (on whom he had looked with great awe only two days before) in a manner and tone which led the worthy tradesman to believe his customer had always been used to command. Once or twice, however, Luke was on the point of breaking down. On purchasing some hose he examined the texture with a minuteness which showed how well he understood such things; and when he saw that Master Longhose was charging him at least fifty per cent. more than the current value of the article, he was all but telling him of the fraud; but he corrected himself in time, and with great magnanimity allowed himself to be swindled. He was at first startled, and then amused, at hearing himself spoken of by his late master. Sir Hubert inquired why they could not be waited on by the fair-complexioned lad he was accustomed to be served by, instead of the clumsy fellow employed. Master Longhose replied that he was in great grief and perplexity about the lad: he had suddenly disappeared and could not be found, although his poor mother was in the greatest distress, and had used every exertion in her power. " It is not only very inconvenient for me," said Master Longhose, " but I am sorry for the lad himself; for he was civil, honest, and industrious, and I have no doubt in time would have risen to be a very respectable tradesman—in a small way."

Their purchases being completed, and ordered to be sent to the " Tabard," Luke and Sir Hubert left the shop. Sir Hubert then proposed they should pay a visit to the horse-dealer's; but Luke asked him rather to recommend him to some house where he could obtain an apartment suitable to his rank. His good-natured acquaintance instantly remembered that a friend of his own, living but a short distance from the Baron of Winterbourne's, was on the point of leaving England for some months on a visit to a relative in Normandy; and he had no doubt he would willingly let Luke his house during the time, and leave his domestics in it also. Luke said such an arrangement would suit him admirably, as he was so much displeased at the laggard behaviour of his own servants that he was determined to send the whole of them back to Scotland the moment they should arrive.

They immediately went to the house, and Luke was struck with the magnificence of the arrangements and the splendour of the servants. The owner, a very extravagant young man, was fortunately at home. The price he asked for his house was enormously high, but Luke took it without hesitation. He further proved his liberality by saying that as he was a stranger he should insist on paying the whole amount in advance, an offer which suited the proprietor admirably. A scrivener was instantly sent for, and in a short time the agreement was drawn up, the money paid, and Luke was to take possession the next day. He then asked Sir Hubert to point out to him his road home, regretting his ignorance of London. Sir Hubert readily did so, and, moreover, proposed calling on his friend in the evening ; but Luke, fearing that play might be again proposed, and knowing that his purse was almost empty, declined the favour, and, instead, invited Sir Hubert to visit him the next day at his new abode. This was agreed on, and Sir Hubert, having put his friend on his way home, bade him good-bye. The remainder of the day Luke spent in purchasing some trunks and travelling necessaries, which he packed up unseen by the people of the inn, and feeling greatly fatigued he went early to bed.

Next morning, on examining his pouch, he

found his purse again filled with gold. After breakfast he called for his host and paid his bill, making most liberal donations to the servants. He then sent for some porters to carry his luggage, and proceeded forthwith to his new residence. The remainder of the morning he spent in making purchases of rich clothes and other articles, all of which he took good care should be at the house previous to the arrival of Sir Hubert. The afternoon he occupied in giving his servants their orders, and making other domestic arrangements, and by the time his friend arrived he was perfectly ready to receive him.

Sir Hubert came alone, and he and Luke passed the evening in conversation together. Sir Hubert again reverted to the subject of the horse, and promised to go with Luke to purchase one the next day, but Luke again postponed it. The fact was he had never been on a horse in his life, and he somewhat dreaded the experiment of mounting one. Sir Hubert then introduced the subject of his own family. He told Luke he lived with the Baron, who would be most happy to make Sir Kenneth Gordon's acquaintance; in fact he had especially commissioned him to tell him so. "The only other person of our family who lives with us," continued Sir Hubert, "is my sister, the Countess de Montereau. She was married some years ago, but the Count died the year after their marriage, and since then she has remained a widow, though she has received several excellent offers from some of the first nobles in England. We keep but little society, as I am sorry to say my father is somewhat out of favour at Court; possibly not without reason, as he is suspected of not being particularly attached to the reigning family. For my own part I take but little interest in politics, and I attend the Court, although I feel I am not much liked there. Of course you intend waiting on the King ? "

Luke replied that he would willingly do so, but, as he had said before, he had no acquaintances in London, and it had been his determination in consequence to preserve a strict incognito. Nevertheless, if he had the opportunity of being presented it would give him considerable pleasure, as he had a great curiosity to see the English Court.

Sir Hubert informed him that nothing would be easier, as he was certain many of his own personal friends would have much pleasure in introducing him.

The conversation again turned on the Baron, and before Sir Hubert quitted the house it was arranged that Luke should dine with him the next day, and he should then have the satisfaction of making him acquainted with his father and sister.

The next day Luke took great pains with his toilet, preparatory to his visit to the Baron's, and it is only doing him justice to say that a handsomer-looking man it would have been difficult to see; and the excellent taste he had shown in his dress set off his figure to the greatest advantage, instead of, as frequently happens, attracting the eye of the observer from it. When the hour for making his visit arrrived, he left his house, and proceeded to the Baron's, feeling rather nervous.

Sir Hubert met him at the door, and immediately conducted him to his father. The Baron was a hale, dignified-looking man, with a peculiar, stern expression of countenance. He received Luke, however, with great friendliness and courtesy, and introduced him to his widowed daughter.

The Countess, though dignified in her manner, was

exceedingly plain in her person, not to say ugly. She was intensely proud, and had also the reputation of possessing a horrible temper. Her servants all detested her, and took no more care in hiding their feelings than the fear of the Baron's chastisement occasioned. The Baron and his daughter received, however, the handsome stranger most favourably, and during the evening behaved to him with marked politeness. At dinner the host and his family noticed their guest's awkward behaviour at table, but attributed it to his Scotch-habits being different from those of Londoners. The evening passed agreeably enough, and it was the commencement of a great friendship between Luke and the Baron's family.

Luke now led a very gay but not a very happy life. He was presented at Court and favourably received; and the houses of many of the nobility, especially those of the same politics as the Baron, were open to him. Without the slightest particle of affection on either side, he had proposed for the hand of the Baron's daughter. He had as yet neither been rejected nor accepted by her, but his suit had not been altogether unfavourably received.

There was only one subject which really gave Luke any annoyance, and that was his mother. Before his good fortune he had been a most affectionate son, but now he had not the slightest love for her. On the contrary he was utterly ashamed of her, and he frequently trembled lest she should meet him and state her relationship. He had not once either called on her or sent her a message since the morning he had left the house in his fine clothes. One afternoon, when returning home (it was almost dark at the time) he met her, and she immediately rushed to meet him with every mark of intense affection. For a moment he was puzzled what to do. At last he pretended he did not know her, but finding that would not do he changed his tactics. With great brutality of tone and manner he told her that in his present position she would be a disgrace to him, and that she must not come near him; if she did he should hand her over to a constable as an impostor. He then took from his purse a couple of gold pieces, and putting them in her hand told her not to trouble him again.

The poor woman, who had stood aghast while he spoke to her, re-covered herself when she felt the gold pieces in her hand. She burst into a violent flood of tears, and throwing the money on the ground left him without uttering another word.

The King, shortly after

Luke's meeting with his mother, ordered a great

hunt in Epping Forest, and Luke, with many others, was invited to attend it. As it would have been disrespectful to have refused his Majesty's invitation, Luke had no alternative but to purchase a horse, which he had hitherto on some excuse or other delayed doing. He got his friend Sir Hubert to go with him to a dealer's, and at last selected one which the dealer said would suit him in every way, and was quite up to his weight. He was ordered to send it the next day to the courtyard at Crosby Palace, where the invited and the courtiers were to meet to accompany the King.

Luke met him at the time appointed, and found his friend Sir Hubert and a crowd of other nobles already assembled. Presently the King appeared, and mounted his horse, and those of his courtiers who were not already in their saddles followed his example. Luke very clumsily mounted his new purchase, a fine magnificent bay, and for a moment sat quietly enough, but no sooner had the King given the order to march than Luke's horse began to caper, probably frightened at the flourish of horns which followed the King's order. Immediately all eyes were upon Luke, and his clumsiness and fright caused a general laugh. Luke heard it and became still more nervous, and at last was thrown from his horse, which galloped rapidly away. The *cortége* then proceeded, still laughing at Luke's misfortune. The King, as he passed him, cruelly said, "Another time, Sir Kenneth, you should bring your nurse with you. I thought you Scotch were better horsemen."

Of course a hearty roar of laughter followed this witticism of the King's, and the cavalcade passed on and left Luke alone.

It would be difficult to describe the shame, anger, and annoyance felt by Luke as he rose from the ground and limped away. He first sought his own house, and there, throwing himself on his bed, vented his rage in vain threats at the King. He remained there in great pain till the evening, when he rose from his bed, and dressing himself in a fresh suit of clothes, he made his way to the house of the Baron of Winterbourne. He found that nobleman and his son in great ill-humour at the little attention shown them by the King at the hunt, and the language they made use of when speaking of their sovereign was scarcely less offensive than that of Luke himself. The result of the whole was that the Baron confided to Luke the particulars of a plot they were hatching against the King, and the rash young man entered into it readily. The conspirators were delighted at having his help, not on account of his talents or influence, but for the ready command of money he seemed to possess.

It would far exceed our limits to go into the particulars of the plot; suffice it to say for some time it progressed favourably for the conspirators, but in the end it was discovered, and Luke, the Baron, Sir Hubert, and about ten others, were

seized and sent to the Tower, on the charge of
High Treason.    There they remained for a week,
when the process commenced against them, and they
were ordered to be examined before the Lord Chief
Justice of the Court of King's Bench.    They were
first questioned separately, and then their depositions
were compared together.    It was impossible, owing
to the number of discrepancies and contradictions
they contained, for the Judge to come to any certain
conclusion as to the amount of culpability of the different offenders, and he therefore ordered that two,
Sir Hubert and Luke, should be placed on the rack
and thus examined.    Sir Hubert's answers, even
under the pain he was suffering, differed but little
from those he had given at his previous examination : not so Luke's.    He contradicted himself a hundred times over, and the sharper the application of
the torture the more he prevaricated, till the surgeon in attendance thought it was impossible for
him to endure more, and he was released.    The result
of the trial was that Sir Hubert, Luke, and two
others, were found guilty, and sentenced to be be-
headed on Tower Hill the next day, the rest being
acquitted.

Terrible was Luke's anguish, both bodily and
mental, that night in his cell.    The punishment
he had undergone still pained him greatly, so much
so that the extreme fear of death he felt could not
distract his attention from it.    He continued thus
till about two o'clock in the morning, when for the

first time his thoughts turned on his mother. He reflected on the great tenderness she had always shown him, and his ingratitude to her when in his prosperity. These thoughts now weighed so heavily on his feelings that he began to cry. He raised his hands to his eyes to wipe away the tears, when on touching his face he found he had no beard. He leaped from his bed in the most intense surprise; and his astonishment was further increased when he felt that his clothes, in which he had lain all night, were of coarse cloth instead of velvet. The enchantment he had been under had been broken, in a way which will be related hereafter. He remained in a state of intense anxiety till dawn, and then he perceived the utter transformation which had been made in his person.

About eight o'clock a warder opened the door of his cell, and without looking in, told him to prepare for execution, and then passed on to open the cell doors of the other prisoners. Luke profited by the opportunity, and slipped noiselessly downstairs into the courtyard. He had been there but a few moments when he was noticed by a warder.

"Hollo, Sir Knave, what are you doing there?"

"I am trying to get out," said Luke, imitating a tone of great simplicity.

"That won't exactly answer without some further explanation. Come here, sir," and he opened the gate of the yard and placed him in his lodge. He there carefully examined him to see if he had stolen

anything, and finding he had nothing on him to the
value of a penny he deliberated for a moment what
he should do with him. Presently it occurred to
him that if it were known a stranger had been
locked in the prisoners' yard all night he might
get himself into trouble for his carelessness. He
then took Luke to the entrance gates, and requested
the soldiers to pommel him well with the staffs of

their halberds, and let him go. The soldiers obeyed
him most conscientiously, and Luke, as soon as he
found himself at liberty, rushed as rapidly as he could
to his mother's house. He felt, as he ran, not the
slightest pain from the torture he had undergone, in
fact it had disappeared at the moment he discovered
his face had no beard on it. He found his mother
at home, and flinging himself on his knees craved
her pardon for his ingratitude, and she, delighted
again to see him, clasped him in her arms and forgave him all the anxiety and grief he had caused her.

## THE MERCHANT'S GOD-DAUGHTER.

MASTER WALTER DE COURCEY had a god-daughter who lived with her mother, the widow of a late Master of the Ironmongers' Company, in the rural village of Newington. Blanche de Courcelle was a pretty piquante girl, about seventeen years of age, of middle height, somewhat dark complexion, and black hair. She was graceful and good-tempered, and was a most dutiful child. Her mother was a tall, angular, middle-aged woman, very religious, but by no means good-tempered. In truth, she led Miss Blanche a very unhappy life, finding fault with everything

she did, and forbidding her every kind of amusement. It may easily be supposed that this was by no means agreeable to the lively, good-tempered girl; but she bore it with much resignation.

Blanche was just at the age when a girl feels the want of a confidant; and, fortunately for her, she had one, though she saw her but seldom, and that was Bertha de Courcey. Blanche's mother, who was not very well off, used to receive her annuity through Master Walter, and for that purpose was accustomed to call on him once every month. On these occasions she took her daughter with her, and they generally dined and spent the day at his house in Bishopsgate. It was on these visits that Blanche opened her heart to Bertha, whom, being two years older, she looked upon almost in the light of a matron. Important and delicate were the secrets then confided, and excellent indeed was the advice Bertha gave her in return, her greater knowledge of the world fully qualifying her for the position of instructress and adviser.

Master Walter himself had little liking for the mother, but he had a great affection for his pretty god-daughter, and from time to time used to make her presents, sometimes of little articles of jewellery, nicknacks, and the other useful things on which young ladies generally set their hearts. But there was one present, above all others, to which Blanche was particularly attached, and that was a beautiful Italian greyhound named Fido. This dog she would never allow to leave her night or day, and it was only her mother's strict orders which could induce her to leave him behind when she went to mass.

To do Fido justice, the affection of his mistress

was warmly reciprocated on his side. He was never happy out of her sight, and apparently never unhappy in it.

When Blanche's mother went to the merchant's and took her daughter with her, they were invariably accompanied by Fido. The mother, who in her heart bore him no love, on these occasions made no objection to his company, and even went so far in Master Walter's presence as to pat him on the head, although she knew perfectly well she ran the risk of having her fingers bitten in return, so little did Fido estimate the high honour done him. Indeed, it was pure maternal feeling on the part of Blanche's mother which caused this mark of affection for the dog when visiting Master de Courcey. In those days, as in these, gratitude consisted in a keen sense of favours to come; and the widow thought, by being fond of Fido when the merchant was present, it might induce him to make her daughter other gifts, and thus her dear child would receive great pleasure and she herself be absolved from the necessity of giving—a weakness to which she was but little addicted.

On the occasion of their last visit to Master Walter, Bertha had just returned from Calais. She was delighted to see her friend, who, on her part, of course, wept tears of joy at again beholding her much-loved confidant. Bertha took Blanche with her into her private chamber, where they talked together for more than an hour, Fido the while sleeping quietly

on his mistress's lap.   Poor Blanche had little to relate to her friend, and that little was by no means
agreeable, being chiefly a record of domestic scenes
and scoldings.   Bertha, on the contrary, had much
to tell.   She related to Blanche the divers adventures she had met with at Calais, the gallantry
of the French, the feasts and balls she had been at,
and a thousand other things highly interesting to
young ladies, but not so much so to the public at large.
But Bertha, when Blanche imagined her to be at the
end of her tale, began to give an account of the visit
of the Count Vicenzio di Garavaglia to her father,
and his subsequent illness and death.   All this was
listened to by Blanche with the greatest interest, but
the climax was to come—the mirror.   Bertha had
expected to see great surprise on the countenance
of her friend, but certainly not to such an extent
as the news produced.   Blanche positively gasped
for breath.   A mirror, and a Venetian one, too!   It
seemed impossible.   Restricted as Blanche's education had been, the fame of the Venetian mirrors had
reached her; but never in her wildest dreams had
she hoped to see one; and now she was positively
under the same roof with a treasure of the kind!

The whole story seemed so utterly marvellous to
Blanche, that she was on the point of accusing her
friend of joking, but courtesy prevented her.

" Do you mean to say, Bertha, that there is a
Venetian mirror in this house ?" she inquired.

" And one of the most beautiful ever manufactured. I am told there is not a king in Europe who possesses one of such size and beauty."

"Oh, how I should like to see it!"

"Some of these days you shall," said Bertha, determined to stimulate her friend's curiosity, if possible.

"And why not to-day, dear? Come, do be a kind, good-natured girl, and let me see it."

Bertha could resist no longer, and she arose from her seat and conducted Blanche, carrying Fido in her arms, into the chamber containing the mirror. When Blanche saw it she was for some moments speechless with admiration. At last she found words.

"Oh, how beautiful it is!" she said. "It is really the handsomest thing in all the world."

"Well," said Bertha, looking at her own reflection in the mirror, "I will not say that, but it is certainly very beautiful."

"Are you not very happy, Bertha, to have it? I know I should be."

"Well," said Bertha, "I should be very sorry to lose it, at any rate."

"Look, Fido," said Blanche, holding him up before it, "look, and see what a little beauty you are."

But Fido seemed but very little impressed with his

own image, for he merely honoured it with a short
bark, and then, turning his head, attempted to lick
his mistress's face.

"Fido is not without taste, I see," said Bertha;
"and I think I know somebody else who would find
more beauty in your face than in the mirror, Blanche.
Bring Osmond here some day and try the experiment."

Blanche merely laughed.  Osmond was the son of
a merchant whose country house was next door to
Blanche's mother's, and who had made himself "very
particular," and had even proposed for her hand, but
had not yet been accepted definitely by the mother.
The families were on terms of great intimacy, however, and he saw her almost daily.  Blanche again
held up Fido, who again turned to his mistress.

"O Fido," she said, clasping him in her arms,
"how I wish you could talk to me!"

"Far better not," said Bertha, "for it would make
Osmond dreadfully jealous, I am sure."

"Oh! I did not mean that anybody else should
understand him," said Blanche; "I only want him
to talk to me."

"That would be more reasonable," said Bertha;
"and it certainly would be much safer than if everybody understood what he said."

The two girls continued talking together for some
time longer, when a message came that Blanche's
mother was about to leave, and Bertha, after locking
the door, accompanied her friend downstairs.

' When Blanche and her mother arrived at home they were both dreadfully fatigued, and they immediately went to bed. Blanche occupied a small room which looked out on the high road, and Fido slept on a bed made up for him by her side. The next morning, when Blanche was dressing, Fido amused himself by standing on a seat looking out of the window and watching the passers-by.

"There goes Osmond," he said, leaping down, "and he never once looked up."

Blanche at the moment thought there must be some other person in the room, and she looked hastily around; but, of course, no one was there. Before she had time to recover herself, Fido said, "I think it was disgraceful of him, knowing, as he does, how fond you are of him."

Blanche now discovered from whence the sound proceeded; she screamed with terror and rushed towards the door for assistance. Fido ran after her, and, leaping up to her, inquired,  "Where are you going, and what are you afraid of?"

Blanche made no answer, but opened the door

ı

and called loudly for her mother, who came to her immediately.

"What is the matter, my dear?"

"O mother, Fido spoke to me!"

"Nonsense, my dear," said her mother, angry at being disturbed.

"But he did, mother."

"What did he say?"

"I did not understand him," said Blanche, colouring slightly; "but he spoke for all that."

"I do not believe a word you say," said her mother; "but if he did we had better send for Father Dunstan the curate. He will either exorcise him, for an evil spirit must be in him, or have him burnt."

Fido uttered a short yell and leaped upon his bed.

"Now, go and dress yourself at once, Blanche, and let us go to mass, and you can talk the matter over with the curate if you like."

So saying, she shut the door, leaving Blanche and Fido together.

"And so, Blanche, you wish to have me burnt?" said Fido.

"For the love of Heaven, who and what are you?" said Blanche.

"I am your poor little dog Fido. I find this morning I can talk, but how I became possessed of the power I know no more than you do."

"But there must be an evil spirit in you, my poor Fido."

"I do not know anything about that," said Fido; "but I hardly think it possible, for I am fonder of you than ever. I think it must be the work of the fairies. At the same time, if you do not wish me to speak, I will never say another word."

Blanche was puzzled what answer to make; she certainly wished Fido to talk, and her fears had begun somewhat to subside.

"But," she said, "if I had no objection, others would hear you talk, and then you would certainly be burnt."

"There is no danger of that," said Fido. "I find I can speak to no one but yourself, and more than that, I am sure no one but you can hear me. If you doubt it, I will speak to you in the presence of your mother, and then you can judge for yourself."

"Very well," said Blanche; "we will try the experiment, and then I will decide afterwards."

Blanche then hastily finished her toilet, and joined her mother in the parlour, where breakfast was set out for them, the old lady having adjourned the idea of going to mass till the morrow, under the pretext that her nerves had been so shaken by the fright Blanche had given her that it would be impossible for her to frame her mind into a proper state for the service.

"Well, Blanche," said her mother, when they were seated at their meal, "I hope you have got over your silly fright of this morning."

"Yes," said Blanche, "I think I have; but I cannot imagine what put it into my head."

"It was no doubt from being over-fatigued yesterday. You will be all right again after breakfast.''

They remained silent for some moments.

"I am sure Osmond is not half so fond of you as I am," said Fido clearly and distinctly.

"What is the matter with that dog to make him whine so?" said the mother.

"I suppose," said Blanche, blushing deeply, "he wants his milk; I will give him some."

"You may well blush," said her mother; "I suppose it was a whine of the kind which frightened you this morning."

Blanche made no remark, but went on with her meal.

After breakfast Blanche took up Fido in her arms and carried him into her chamber. When she had closed the door, Fido said,

"I told you no one could understand me but yourself, and I am sure you are now convinced I spoke the truth. Now listen to what I propose. Keep my secret. If ever you hear me utter one wrong word, or anything that might injure you, hand me over to the curate if you please. If I do not, you may be certain there is no evil spirit in me. Besides, I think I may be of great use to you, in giving you good advice, which will always be for your benefit, for I am sure there is no one in the world fonder of you than I am."

"Very well," said Blanche; "on those terms I will keep your secret."

In the afternoon Blanche walked out with her mother for the purpose of making some visits to their neighbours. Blanche talked but little, as her mind was fully occupied with Fido. For some time she was greatly in doubt whether she was right in keeping the secret, but upon further consideration came to the conclusion that Fido was gifted by the fairies, and as fairies did not rank as evil spirits, she could be doing no wrong. She then turned her thoughts on Osmond, to whom she was tenderly attached. She was somewhat annoyed, however, at his not looking up at her casement when he passed in the morning, and she resolved that when he called next time she would as a punishment receive him very coldly, and thus show him that she would allow no slight to be played on her with impunity. She had had the discretion during her visits to leave Fido behind her, who remained sulking in her chamber the while.

In the evening Osmond, after his return from the City, called on them, and was received very graciously by the mother, and very coldly by the daughter, who sat moodily on her seat with Fido on her lap. The conversation for some time was carried on on general subjects. At last the mother asked Osmond if there was any news in the City.

"Everybody," said he, "is talking of the magnificent ball the King is going to give."

"When is it to take place?" asked the mother.

"In about a fortnight. It is to be one of the grandest sights that have been seen in London for many a day; and your friend," he continued, turning to Blanche, "Bertha de Courcey, will be one of the stars of the evening."

"And I suppose," said Blanche, somewhat spitefully, "you would like to be with her?"

"Indeed I should," said Osmond. "It would give me very great pleasure; and as the families of several of the Aldermen will be invited, and as my father is one, perhaps, after all, I may have a chance of meeting her. I should like immensely to dance with Bertha."

"Do you hear that?" said Fido; "he must be very fond of you, certainly."

"Blanche, my dear," said her mother, "you must turn that dog out of the room. His whining is insufferable, and it shakes my nerves to pieces. Take him away directly," and Fido immediately afterwards found himself a prisoner in Blanche's bedroom, where he occupied himself in informing the moon, which he saw through the casement, in genuine canine howls, of the shameful treatment he was receiving.

When Blanche returned to the sitting-room, she continued silent and wayward; nor could any attempts of her lover put her into better humour. Finding all his efforts had no effect on her, he took up his cap at a much earlier hour than usual, and wishing mother and daughter good night, he left the house.

No conversation passed between Fido and his mistress that night. She spoke to him kindly once or twice, but he simply coiled himself round, and tucking his nose under him, pretended he was sleepy. In fact, he was simply sulky, and instead of going to sleep he occupied his Italian brains in inventing a plot to cause a quarrel between Osmond and Blanche. Of the former he was exceedingly jealous, and of the latter he was immensely fond. It was not long before he had concocted a most diabolical plot, and having arranged it to his perfect satisfaction, he went really to sleep.

When Blanche rose the next morning, and was occupied at her toilet, she cast from time to time sly glances at the high road to see if Osmond should look up as he passed. Fido placed himself on the stool at the window, also watching for the young fellow, but with no friendly intentions. Presently, when Blanche was occupied at the back of the room, Fido leaped from his seat, and with much indignation in his tone said,

"Upon my honour, this is too bad. That fellow Osmond has passed again without looking up. It is really disgraceful, considering how you love him."

Now the whole of this was a lie. Osmond not only looked up, but he had positively stood some moments before the house to catch a glimpse of his sweetheart.

"I wish," said Blanche, somewhat spitefully, "you would not always be amusing yourself at the window; one would think you were a housemaid."

"I am very sorry," said Fido, "and I will not do it again.  I was not looking for Osmond, but for somebody I like much better."

"And pray who may he be?"

"Doctor Thomas, the leech.  If I were a young girl," said Fido, "he would be the man for my money."

"Doctor Thomas, indeed!" said Blanche, with a sneer.  "Why, he's sixty if he is a day."

"Fifty-eight, at the out·side," said Fido.  "Not an hour more, I assure you."

We must here state, to make the present conversation between Fido and his mistress intelligible, that Doctor Thomas was a wealthy old widower, who greatly admired Blanche, but who had received no encouragement from her whatever.

"I don't care," said Blanche, "whether he is fifty-eight or twenty-eight; but I would have nothing to say to him if he were Lord Mayor."

"*Vedremo*," said Fido to himself in his native language.

Fido now began preparations for his diabolical

plot. By cunningly insinuating himself into Blanche's confidence, he had induced her to persuade her mother to invite Osmond, and his father and mother, and Doctor Thomas to spend an evening together at her house. Before the time of their meeting had arrived, Fido, with the spirit of an Iago, had contrived to make Blanche horribly jealous, by means of lies he had invented, detailing expressions of admiration he said he had at different times heard the young fellow express about Bertha. All this he did so artfully that, when the evening of the party arrived, it was with great difficulty that Blanche could keep her temper in Osmond's presence. To annoy him, however, she paid the greatest attention to Dr. Thomas, thereby again resuscitating hopes which he had considered extinct. He showed himself exceedingly flattered at the notice she took of him, and behaved to her with such ease and graceful gallantry, as would have led anyone to suppose he could not have exceeded forty.

With Osmond, on the contrary, affairs were very different. He sat sorrowful and silent on his seat, not saying a word, and looking the very picture of despair. Sorrow sat well upon his handsome features, and, to Fido's intense annoyance, made him look vastly interesting, which even Blanche, with all her ill-humour, was obliged to admit. After a very dull evening the guests left, Blanche taking a very friendly leave of the Doctor, and utterly forgetting to say good-night to Osmond.

When Blanche had entered her chamber, Fido said to her, "Call Osmond a lover, indeed! I never in my life saw a man pay less attention to the girl of his choice than he did to you. I don't know whether that is the method of expressing affection in England, but in my country it is very different."

All the answer he received, however, was, "Lie down, naughty dog;" a sentence which appeared to annoy him exceedingly, and he did not recover his good temper till breakfast time the next morning.

As the time advanced Fido's love for his mistress and his hatred for Osmond increased. He determined to carry out his plot and thus break off the contemplated match. He calculated that if Blanche married Osmond she would no longer care about him, while if she married Dr. Thomas there could be but little affection on her part, and there would remain abundant space in her heart for attachment to him. But at the same time he knew human nature, dog as he was, sufficiently well to be aware that some accidental circumstance might bring about a reconciliation between Blanche and Osmond, and that it was his policy, now that he had effected a breach in their loves, to widen it to such an extent as to leave no possibility of its being healed. After much thought, he formed a scheme which could only have emanated from the brain of a wicked dog, and an intriguing Italian dog into the bargain.

One morning, seeing Blanche very low-spirited, he said to her,

" It really grieves me exceedingly to see you look so sad. I am sure I would willingly do all I could to make peace between you and Osmond, if I were only assured that he really loves you."

" I am sincerely obliged to you," said Blanche, gratefully. " If I could only be certain of that I would make up my mind at once; but how am I to arrive at the truth?"

" I have thought of a plan," said Fido. " Your mother has not for some time had one of her nervous headaches. It will certainly come on to-morrow or the next day at the latest. When she is at the worst, which is generally in the afternoon, I will set up a fearful whining, for which you must scold me soundly. I will, however, not be quiet, but on the contrary, break out into a regular howl. 'Fido,' you must say, ' I can stand this no longer. I cannot allow mamma to be annoyed in this manner. I must take you out of the house.' You must then put on your cloak and coif, and take me to Osmond's mother's, and tell her that as your own mother is very ill, and cannot bear the noise of the dog, you would be very much obliged to her if she would take charge of me for the night. Of course she cannot refuse, and while I am there I will listen to all that passes, and let you know everything when you fetch me away the next morning."

Blanche, we are sorry to say, made herself a party

to this abominable plot. Everything fell out exactly
as Fido prognosticated; and the morning after her
mother's sick headache she went to fetch back the dog.
When she saw him she took him in her arms and
kissed him affectionately; then thanking Osmond's
mother for her kindness, she left her to return home.

She had hardly got to her own chamber, and closed
the door, when Fido began,

" O my poor mistress, how much I pity you!
What a nest of vipers you have to do with! I had on
several occasions the greatest difficulty in restraining
myself from flying at the throat of that old woman.
Would you believe it, she is trying all she can to get
up a match between Osmond and Bertha, with whom
he is desperately in love ?  She however advises him
to keep on with you till he knows the result of his
suit with Bertha, as she doesn't think you'd make a
bad wife after all, although she doesn't much like
you.  But he says if he cannot have Bertha, he will
have nobody else; he's thoroughly tired of you as it
is, and that he tried to show it to you when he was
last here."

We need hardly say the whole of Fido's statement
was an abominable lie.  Poor Blanche when she
heard it wept bitterly, and her eyes were so red that
she could not go down to dinner.  She requested
the servant to ask her mother to excuse her, as
she in her turn had a violent headache, and was
obliged to lie down on her bed.  Fido remained with
his mistress to console her.  When he found she

was somewhat calmer, he introduced the subject of
Dr. Thomas, and pleaded his cause so warmly that
Blanche became suspicious, and at last, raising herself
on her elbow and re-
garding him sternly in
the face, said to him
with much solemnity of
tone,

"Fido, he has been
bribing you with pieces
of sugar."

"On my honour as a dog," said Fido, "he has
done nothing of the kind. You wound me dreadfully
with your base suspicions."

And here he set up such a fearful howl that Blanche
was fain to apologise and promise to believe him for
the future if he would be silent.

But Fido, notwithstanding all his duplicity, did
not get all his own way with his mistress. She
determined to wait till the ball was over. If Osmond
went to it, and made an offer to Bertha, she would
never have anything to say to him, but accept Dr.
Thomas, who had now proposed in due form. Although this arrangement by no means pleased Fido,
he was obliged to consent to it; but he had the cunning to propose that he should be left at Osmond's
mother's again the night of the ball, and then he
could inform Blanche the next day of all that had
taken place, as no doubt the mother and son would
talk it over at breakfast. In the mean time the

health of Blanche began to fail her from the anxiety she suffered, so much so, in fact, that even her own mother, albeit not particularly quick at distinguishing ill health in anybody but herself, became alarmed at it, and she talked over the matter with Osmond's mother, who really seemed extremely sorry for the poor girl.

We must now leave Blanche and her history till after the ball, when we will again bring her under the notice of the reader.

# V

# THE SACRISTAN OF ST. BOTOLPH.

MASTER WALTER DE COURCEY, although an indefatigable man of business, was extremely punctual in his religious observances, and he made a point, both in winter and summer, of attending early mass in his parish church, St. Botolph's, Bishopsgate. It has already been stated that his departure for Windsor was very sudden, in fact hardly any one out of his own house was aware that he had left London. The officiating priest at the church was therefore much surprised at his non-appearance two days running; and as Master Walter did not appear on the third, nor in fact for a week, he began to fear he might be indisposed, and one morning, as soon as mass was over, he directed the sacristan to call at the merchant's house and inquire after his health. The sacristan was a certain Geoffrey Cole, a very tall thin man with a low forehead, deep sunk eyes, harsh features, and very large hands and feet. Although something of a miser, intensely selfish, and most uncharitable, both in the matter of giving alms, and in his feelings

towards his neighbours, he was extremely puncti-
lious in all the external forms and ceremonies of the

Church, and he flattered himself
he was not only very religious, but
even a model of piety. The more
he studied the subject, the more
certain of his blissful state he became, till at last he believed himself to be so good that the saints
alone were his equals. He would
frequently draw comparisons between his life and some of the inferior saints, and he generally concluded he could compare with them
most advantageously. On the morning when he was directed to call on
Master Walter this train of thought
especially occupied his mind, and
by the time he had arrived at the house he was certain that in the whole city of London there was not
another individual so good as himself.

The person who received him was an old woman
half imbecile from age, who had formerly been
Master Walter's nurse, and with her the sacristan
had frequently conversed on matters of what he called
religion. When he had received from her an explanation of the merchant's absence from church, the
pair commenced talking on subjects connected with
Church affairs, which consisted in fact of the sacristan's explaining to her what a good and pious man he

was, and her complimenting him thereon. Before he
left the house the nurse asked him if he would like
to see the mirror, as she would have much pleasure
in showing it to him. He accepted the offer at once, at
the same time saying that vanities of the kind had
but few attractions for him.

The nurse led the way to the chamber, and
when they had arrived there, in spite of his mock
ascetic manner, there was no difficulty in perceiving
he admired the mirror greatly. Fearing, however,
the real state of his mind might be detected by the
old woman, he began to speak of it in terms of great
disparagement, not indeed finding fault with its form
and beauty, but dwelling on the absurdity of mortals
setting their minds on such trifles, and neglecting
subjects of far greater importance which concerned
the welfare of their souls.

"But everybody cannot be so good as you are,
Master Geoffrey," said the old woman; "and you
ought to have a little feeling for those who are not."

"I do not see that," said the sacristan, taking the
compliment without the slightest hesitation. "I con-
demn all trifles of the kind. What would the blessed
St. Anthony have said to a vanity of this sort?"

"Ah!" said the old woman; "but it would not
be possible in the present day to find so good a man
as he was."

"It would be very difficult, I admit," said the
sacristan; "but I am not sure it would be impossible.
Do not think for a moment that I would attempt to

compare myself with him; but I thought, while
reflecting on his life as I came here this morning, that
I should very much like to be subjected to the same
temptations, to see if I could not resist them."

"You surely do not mean that?" said the nurse;
" why, they were dreadful."

" Indeed, I do," said the sacristan, looking at himself in the mirror, " I should like immensely to be
subjected to them for a month, and then I could form
an idea whether I was as good as I ought to be."

" Well," said the nurse, leaving the room with
him, " I trust you will never be subjected to anything of the kind."

After a little conversation of the same description
the sacristan left the house.

After he had delivered his message to the priest
and the functions of the day were over, he sought his

own home in the rural district of Little Moorfields. He lived in a room on the top floor of a house occupied by a man and his wife who were employed at a merchant's house in the City. As the merchant and his family were absent, Geoffrey's landlord and his wife were requested to sleep at the house of business, and thus he had for the time the whole abode to himself.

His room, which was comfortably furnished, was the very picture of neatness and cleanliness, for he was very particular in his domestic arrangements; and his landlady, during her temporary absence at the house of business, called every day to put his room in order, and place his supper on the table.

Arrived at home he requested a neighbour's wife to light his lamp and fire for him, and that being done she left him. He then bolted the street door, went up to his own room, and after a very comfortable and abundant meal went to bed, having, however, left ample food on the table for his breakfast the next morning. He was generally a very sound sleeper, and his slumbers that night formed no exception to the general rule; but, somehow or other, as morning advanced they were by no means so profound. He grew very restless, with a sense of oppression, and occasionally he heard a sound like the tinkling of a bell, which continued till daybreak, when the annoyance became intolerable. At last, when it was fully day, he aroused himself and sat up in his bed. What was his surprise and terror

when he saw, stretched across the foot of it, outside
the clothes, a large fat pig with a bell fastened round

its neck with a leathern strap.    His first attempt was
to push the brute from the bed, but the only effect
produced was that it placed itself in a still more
comfortable position directly on his legs, and then
went to sleep again.    Enraged and in great pain, he
immediately began to pommel the pig with his fist on
the neck and head, but without other result than a
few surly grunts.    His passion increased to such an
extent that he struck it still harder blows, when
suddenly his attention was arrested by a loud peal of
laughter, and he saw, sitting on his stool by the fire-
place, an imp so intensely ugly that he was almost
frightened to look at it.    Somewhat recovering himself, he said, " Who are you, and what are you doing
here ?"

"No matter who I am," said the imp; "but as to what I am doing, I am simply laughing at your ungrateful and absurd behaviour."

"In what way," said the sacristan, "is my behaviour absurd?"

"In attacking in that violent manner your friend and pig."

"My pig?" said the sacristan; "I have no pig. It is none of mine."

"O you ungrateful man," said the imp. "Did you not yesterday say you wished you could meet with some temptations similar to

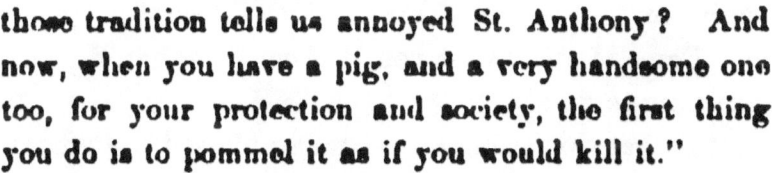

those tradition tells us annoyed St. Anthony? And now, when you have a pig, and a very handsome one too, for your protection and society, the first thing you do is to pommel it as if you would kill it."

"I did not know it was a pig of that description," said the sacristan, with much solemnity of tone, "or I should have treated it with the respect it deserves."

"Well, then, do so now," said the imp; "to all appearance it will give you ample opportunity for a trial of patience."

"But I cannot remain here all day," said the sacristan, "I must go to my duties; I shall be scolded as it is for being too late."

Then scratching the pig lovingly on the poll, he

addressed it with much sweetness of tone and manner : "If it is not asking you too great a favour, would you oblige me by getting off my bed ? I am really very sorry to trouble you, but you are rather heavy, and I suffer from corns."

But the pig took no further notice of these blandishments than closing its eyes more fast than ever, and falling into a sounder sleep.

"What am I do ?" said the poor sacristan, in a despairing tone.

"Exercise your patience," said the imp. "He is affording you capital practice."

The sacristan was now silent, and for some time the imp said nothing, contenting himself with a quiet chuckle. Presently, however, he said to the sacristan,

"Come, I will assist you if I can. What do you want me to do ?"

"To get this accurs——I mean blessed pig off my bed if you can."

"I can do it easily enough," said the imp ; "but you mortals are so ungrateful, it is ten to one you will be angry with me if I do."

"On the contrary," said Geoffrey, "I shall be most grateful to you, I promise you on my word of honour. That is to say," he continued, "if it do not put the dear creature to much pain."

"I promise you that it shall, on the contrary, be much pleased."

"Pray proceed then."

The imp immediately leaped off the stool, and going to the table took from it the food the sacristan had set aside for his breakfast, and placing it on the ground called out, " Pig, pig."

The pig lazily opened its eyes and looked on the ground. No sooner, however, did it see the food than its sleepy fit left it, and it jumped from the bed and com-

menced a furious attack on the sacristan's breakfast.

Master Geoffrey, in spite of his promise, was now dreadfully angry. He leaped on the floor, and rushing to the pig attempted in vain to push it away from the food, the imp laughing lustily the while.

" Upon my word," he said, " I never saw in my life a man worse adapted for an anchorite than you are. Why, you ought to be delighted to see your pig enjoy itself so heartily."

Master Geoffrey immediately left the pig and cast a very proper look of intense hatred at the imp, who seemed more delighted with it than ever.

" Did I not tell you," he said, " that you would be ungrateful to me for my kindness?"

The sacristan made no reply, but commenced dressing himself. He went on systematically with his toilet, casting occasionally an envious glance at the pig, but by the time he was fully dressed he had contrived to regain his equanimity. He now put on his cap as if to leave the house, and then going to the pig, he patted it on the back and scratched its head, saying at the time,

"There's a good pig, go on with your breakfast, and when you have finished we will take a pretty pleasant walk together down to St. Botolph's, and there I will leave you in the streets till my duties are over, and then we will walk back together comfortably in the evening."

Here the imp set up a furious laugh, and stamped on the floor with pleasure.

"Bravo! admirable!" he said; "upon my word you are a nice fellow. You know the Lord Mayor has lately published an order that all pigs found in the streets of the City shall have their throats cut, and their flesh given to the poor. Upon my word you are a very clever fellow, and I begin to like you immensely. I could not have done anything better myself."

Master Geoffrey contented himself with casting another look of intense hatred at the imp, but he said nothing.

After a few minutes' silence the imp said to him, "Now I know you want to ask me a question and are too proud to do it. You would inquire what you must do with the pig during the day?"

"I acknowledge it," said the sacristan. "What can I do with it?—of course I cannot take it to the church with me."

" Leave it at home, then. I should if I were you, rather than be bothered with it all day."

" Well, I should like to do that, but if my land-lady should come and find it here she would very likely drive it away. Perhaps," he said, after a moment's reflection, " that would be the better way after all."

" Not at all," said the imp, " it would be sure to find its way back again at night, so that would be of no use. I see you want to get rid of it."

" Your base suspicions annoy me."

" Indeed. Now let me advise you. Go round to the house your landlady lives at, and tell her that you do not want your room arranged either to-day or to-morrow. She will be pleased to hear it, as I know she is suffering very severely from an attack of rheumatism. So you see you can leave the pig in your room without the slightest danger of its being found out by anyone. Now you had better go. Do not forget to bring the pig's supper back with you, or it will again be under the unpleasant necessity of eating that which you had reserved for yourself. Now good-bye."

The sacristan then left the house, and after having called on his landlady and assured her that there would be no occasion for her to arrange his room for him either that day or the next,—a piece of news which gave her great satisfaction, as the weather was cold and her rheumatism worse,—he continued his way to the church, where he had great difficulty in

making his peace with the priest for being so late.
When the duties of the day were over, he first went
to an eating-house and eat a most hearty supper,
determining that the pig should not deprive him
of that meal.   He then bought sufficient for his
breakfast the next morning, and afterwards some
vegetables for the pig.   This last investment, we are
obliged to acknowledge with great sorrow, caused
him much annoyance.   He had a violent objection
to spend money on anybody but himself, and
although he wished to act up to the part of an
anchorite as closely as he could, he never had
heard of one spending money on a dumb animal,
and he almost considered it to be a work of supereroga-
gation to waste the money he had done on the pig.
However, it was done, and there was no help for
it.   He sincerely repented his fault, and he could
say no more; he would be more cautious another
time.

When he arrived at home and had procured a light
from a neighbour, he entered his room and found in
it the pig and the imp.   He showed little delight at
the sight of either.   The pig, on the contrary,
received him with every mark of satisfaction, that
is to say, as soon as it perceived the vegetables
under the sacristan's arm.

The sacristan took no notice of the imp, but
threw the vegetables down on the floor, setting
aside, however, enough for the pig's breakfast the
next morning, and it was soon occupied with its

supper. The sacristan watched it thoughtfully as it fed, not a word being spoken the while either by the imp or himself.

When the pig was fully satisfied, the sacristan swept up the remains, and opening the casement threw them into the street. He then closed it quickly as the weather was cold, intending to enjoy, if possible, a comfortable night's rest, when, to his intense horror, he found the pig had leaped upon the bed and had stretched itself full length upon it from head to foot, so that it would have been difficult for the sacristan to have placed himself beside the pig even if he had been so inclined.

The sacristan could hardly contain his rage, indeed for a moment it partially broke out, but a roar of laughter from the imp induced him to restrain himself. With great difficulty he put something like an amiable smile on his countenance, and then addressed the pig with much genuine persuasion in his tone and manner.

"Come off the bed, there's a good pig," he said, "and I will make you up another on the floor, where you will be much more comfortable than you are

there.  Come now, there's a good pig."  But the
only answer he got was a grunt.

"What in the name of Fortune," said the imp,
"do you want the pig to get off the bed for?"

"Why to sleep there myself, of course," said the
sacristan.

"Upon my word, you are a pretty anchorite.
You slept like a top all last night to my certain
knowledge, and you want to go to bed to-night!"

"What am I expected to do then?" said the
sacristan.

"Pass the night in meditation on the floor, of
course; who ever heard of an anchorite sleeping two
nights running?  You will now find how invaluable
is your pig.  It will sleep soundly enough while you
meditate, but the moment you fall asleep it will ring

its bell. I see you do not like that arrangement, and I begin to suspect you are no better than a sham after all."

"I will prove to you I am," said the sacristan; "that is to say if I am to have the pleasure of your company here all night."

"That you will not have," said the imp, "but you will see me in the morning," and he immediately vanished.

To say the truth, the sacristan passed a most uncomfortable night. Whenever he attempted to sleep, the pig rang its bell until the unfortunate man was fully awake, and then went to sleep himself. Several times in the course of the night did he beg the pig to keep quiet, and once he endeavoured to explain to it that he always meditated best with his eyes shut, but the pig would hear of no compromise, and continued faithfully to do its duty till morning. When day broke the imp made his appearance, and as before seated himself on the stool.

"What sort of a night have you passed?" said the imp.

"A very unpleasant—I mean a very happy one, indeed."

"I do not believe you," said the imp. "I suspect after all you are not the man to resist temptation."

"There you are certainly wrong," said the sacristan. "No man," he continued, casting a most vindictive glance at the pig, "was ever more cruelly tempted than I have been to-night, and yet I successfully resisted it. But after all I candidly admit that, all things considered, it will be exceedingly difficult for me to carry out my wish at present, much as it would disappoint me to relinquish it. You must perceive yourself that in a small room like this, I have no convenience or accommodation for a temptation of the kind."

" O you coward ! " said the imp. " What, going to give in already ? No accommodation indeed ! Why, I should like to know how the anchorites of old managed ? "

" They had the desert handy, where they had plenty of room."

" Why do you not go there then ? "

" How absurdly you talk !" said the sacristan peevishly. " Why, the desert is so far off it would take me a life-time to get there."

" Try Kennington Common, then," said the imp. " There will be room enough for you there, and I observed the other day at the farthest part a half-ruined shed that would serve you and your pig admirably for shelter."

" If I went there," said the sacristan, " would it be necessary for me to take the pig with me ? "

" Of course; its duty is to keep you from relapsing ; and besides that, it would not stay behind though you wished it."

The sacristan reflected for some minutes. To say the truth, the proposition of the imp did not altogether displease him. Near that part of Kennington

Common resided a buxom widow very well to do in the world, who was rather fond of hearing the sacristan converse on serious subjects. He calculated that if bad weather came on, or if his provisions did not hold out, or if he were cold or dull, he could go to her house and instruct her.

"I think," said he at last to the imp, "your idea an excellent one, and I will carry it out. As soon as my duties for the day are over, I will go to the Common and remain there a week at least, that is to say, if the priest will give me leave of absence for so long a time, of which I have little doubt. I will go immediately and ask him."

So saying he left the house, after giving the pig its breakfast.

In the evening the sacristan returned to the house with a large bundle of warm clothing, some boiled bacon and ham, and bread enough to last him for several days, which he placed on the table, and a very small quantity of food for the pig, which he threw on the ground, and on which the pig began to feed ravenously. The sacristan then seated himself on the bed to recover his breath, for he was greatly fatigued with the exercise he had taken.

"What may those things be for?" said the imp, pointing to the bundle on the table.

"It is warm clothing," said the sacristan, "for the nights are cold."

"That is hardly *en règle*," said the imp; "you ought to take nothing more with you than you have

on.   The ancient anchorites never had even a change
of linen."

"You forget," said the sacristan, "they lived in
warmer climates, where it was not required; here,
where it is colder, it would be allowed.   I have well
studied that question, and I know I am right."

"And that other parcel, what may that contain?"

"Boiled bacon and ham, and bread."

"That is not orthodox."

"Why not?"

"If you are going to live the life of an anchorite,
you must live upon herbs and roots, and drink nothing but water; and, by-the-bye, if I am not mistaken, I see something in your bundle the form of
which is remarkably like that of a leathern bottle of
wine."

"I have received a dispensation from the priest to
eat meat for the next fortnight, and the wine is to be
taken occasionally on account of my weak state of
health."

"You hypocrite!" said the imp; "you have
imposed on the worthy priest.   You know there is
nothing the matter with you."

"I scorn your imputation," said the sacristan with
much virtuous indignation in his tone; "I have practised no imposition on the holy man whatever.   I
went to a leech and told him I felt in a very weak
state of health, and I gave him a crown to give me a
certificate that a course of animal food with wine was
necessary for me, and this certificate I took to the

priest, who, on the faith of it, gave me the dispensation. If there is any sin in the matter it is the doctor's, not mine—I took good care of that."

" Upon my word," said the imp, " I begin to respect you. You are evidently a man after my own heart."

" I consider your hatred," said the sacristan, " a far greater compliment than your love."

.The sacristan now made preparations for his journey, and left the house with the pig.

" *Bon voyage*," said the imp ; but he received no answer.

The sacristan and the pig made their way without much difficulty through the City, and even crossed the crowded thoroughfare of London Bridge without anything occurring particularly worthy of remark. When they arrived at the Borough Market things did not go on so well. The pig had had but a very scanty supper, and the quantity of vegetables he found strewed about in the market offered an amount of temptation he could not resist. The market at the time was crowded, and the pig, in its eagerness to obtain food, ran in the way of the merchants and purchasers, and in return got many and sundry hard kicks, which appeared not to agree with its constitution.

It is well known that even the best pigs, when hungry, have but little of the moral quality of integrity about them, and the one whose history we are recording formed no exception to the rule. Not content with picking up the refuse vegetables

L

which lay strewn about, it had the imprudence to
walk off with a fine cauliflower from a trader's
basket.   This was perceived, however, and the hue
and cry was immediately raised.   The cauliflower was

taken from it, and a perfect shower of kicks was
rained on its sides.   Some inquired to whom the pig
belonged, and one asked the sacristan if it was his.
We are sorry to be obliged to say that he replied in
the negative, and still more sorry to admit that while
his pig was being assaulted in this cruel manner, he
looked on without the slightest expression of indignation or compassion on his face, and at last turned
on his heel and continued his road, letting his pig
disengage itself from the crowd as it best could.

He had hardly arrived at Newington when the pig
joined him, grunting in a most lamentable manner.
At last the pair reached Kennington Common, and
the sacristan made directly for the shed mentioned by
the imp.   He found it without any difficulty, and without allowing the pig time to make a choice, he appropriated the driest and warmest corner to himself.

The pig offered no opposition, for the treatment it had received appeared to have taken every particle of courage out of it, and it threw itself down in an opposite corner, and was soon fast asleep. The sacristan now undid his wallet, and, after having made a hearty supper, he put on some warm clothing and went to sleep, having first hung his wallet and provisions under the roof so as to be out of the reach of the pig.

Next morning he found the imp in the shed, but the pig had sauntered out for the moment into a neighbouring turnip-field.

"So you arrived here safely?" said the imp to the sacristan, who was occupied with his break-fast. "I followed you under the form of a dog the whole of the way, and I must say your conduct was most cow-ardly and disgraceful. You looked on with perfect indifference when that pig was  being so horribly maltreated in the market."

"That is not true," said the sacristan; "I assure you that I felt bitterly for the poor animal. I felt as much pain from every kick it received as if it had been inflicted on my own person; but I said to myself, Here is a trial for me, and it is my duty to support it meekly and with patience. And I flatter myself I did so admirably. When the kicks were being showered so cruelly on its sides I not only made no opposition, but, wishing to see how far my own self-denial would go, I said, Kick on."

"And, pray, why did you deny being its master?"

"That I might not appear proud. Pride is a sin I despise."

"Capital! Now, what do you intend to do this morning?—meditate, I suppose?"

"No," said the sacristan with a sigh; "I would willingly do so, but unfortunately I am unable. I have occasion to go into the City."

"Nonsense, you know you have got leave of absence for a fortnight, and there is no occasion whatever for you to go there."

"You are in error," said the sacristan mildly, "for go I must."

"Might I ask on what errand?"

"To get some wine."

"How preposterous!" said the imp; "you brought enough with you to last a moderate man for three days at least."

"Not under the circumstances in which I was placed," said the sacristan. "You forget how cold it was."

"What, in the name of Fortune, has that to do with it? Do you think the anchorites of old drank wine in that manner?"

"Possibly not, very possibly not; but their case

was very different. They did not suffer from cold, for they lived in a warm climate. I do not, and I am justified in taking as much wine while living in this open shed as shall raise the temperature of my body to an equality with that of theirs in the African desert; and that cannot be done under a bottle a day. Now I have only one leathern bottle in my possession, and therefore you yourself must perceive that I am obliged, though sorely against my inclination, to go to London every day."

"That is very sad indeed," said the imp; "but do you not think the anchorites, had they been placed in your position, would have attempted to abstain from wine? Judging from what I have heard of them, I think they would."

"I do not agree with you. Judging from my own conscientious feelings on the subject, I am decidedly of opinion they would not; nor will I try it, lest I might fall into a grievous and sinful error."

"And what may that be?"

"In thinking that so sinful a mortal as I am could surpass the sanctity of those venerable men. I am not sure that even making the attempt would not be a mortal sin, and I shall not try it."

"Just as you please," said the imp. "When do you start?"

"Immediately. Now, my faithful companion," he continued, addressing the pig, who had just returned from the turnip-field, where, judging from the rotundity of its person, it had made an excellent breakfast, "let us start off for London at once, that we may have plenty of time to see the sights; that is to say, after I have called on a friend of mine who lives in St. Nicholas in the Shambles."

But the pig took no notice of the invitation, and stolidly prepared a bed for itself in the corner of the shed. Doubtless a vivid reminiscence of the Borough Market,—through which it would have to pass,—was still fresh in its memory.

It was nearly dark when the sacristan returned to the shed that evening. He appeared in perfect good humour with himself and all the world; and if his cheeks were not rosy his nose was certainly slightly so. Altogether he presented the appearance of a person who had drunk a trifle more than was absolutely necessary for him, without being at all intoxicated. He hung up a bottle of wine under the roof, with some ham and some bread, and then, seating himself in his corner, he attempted to meditate, but did not succeed. He felt that evening especially the want of society, for even the pig lay fast asleep beside him, after a hearty supper in the turnip-field. He would have felt more comfortable if the imp had been there, although expressly sent to tempt him. The feeling of *ennui* grew on him till he found it almost insupportable, and at last he determined, although it was rather late in the day for a person connected with the church to call upon a lone woman, to pay the widow a visit, and talk with her on moral subjects. The resolution was no sooner formed than he rose from his seat to put it in practice, and putting his cap on his head in a jaunty manner, he left the house.

To his sore annoyance, however, the pig, which had been as still as a dormouse while he was in the shed, showed unusual signs of liveliness when he quitted it. It rose up, and, following him, gambolled round in front of him, impeding his walk, and grunt- ing and ringing its bell in a most absurd manner. This enraged him excessively, for although he had nothing to be ashamed of in visiting the widow, still, when a man calls on the

woman of his choice, he does not wish it to be trumpeted forth to all the world, in such a very ridiculous manner. He attempted to drive the pig back again without the slightest effect, and we are sorry to add made use of such language on the occasion as any well-disposed sacristan would be shocked to repeat. At the same time it is but just to state that, when he found he could not get the pig to forego its intention by any possible entreaties and threats, he honestly begged its pardon, and allowed it to accompany him.

When they arrived at the widow's door the pig placed itself close against it, so as to be able to enter at the same time with its master. This annoyed the sacristan exceedingly; of course he could not allow the pig to enter, yet how to keep it out he did not know. The widow, who was rather of a timorous disposition, called out before opening the door, "Who's there?"

The sacristan immediately answered that it was he, and that there was a pig outside which seemed desirous to enter. Was it hers?

"No," she said; "pray drive it away."

"I have tried to do so," said the sacristan, "but I have not succeeded."

"Wait a moment, I will see what I can do;" and a minute afterwards the widow opened the door.

Armed with a besom, she dealt the pig a tremendous blow on the snout.

Now it is well known that a pig, which may be as bold as a lion on all other occasions, will not face a housewife with a besom. So the sacristan's pig started back, and howled terribly, while its master, profiting by its retreat, entered the house.

The sacristan found a warm, blazing fire in the widow's little sitting-room, and the table was spread out for her solitary supper. The place had a look of comfort about it which directly went to his heart, and he regretted that so amiable a person should have no one always at hand to talk to her on serious subjects, and advise her in the management of her affairs. She appeared much pleased to see him, the more so as that evening she had been reflecting on her solitary lot. She immediately placed another platter on the table, and produced some wine, which she kept by her to use medicinally, as occasion required. The sacristan was touched by her kindness. In return he talked to her very comfortably, showing

her the folly of setting one's heart on sublunary things, and doing full justice to her provisions the while. He would have been perfectly happy had it not been for the incessant ringing of the pig's bell outside the house. The widow, in the course of conversation, asked him what he was doing in that out-of-the-way part of the world. He told her he had requested leave of absence from his priest, and that during it he was determined to pass the time in meditation amid the solitude of the Common. She admired his resolution, and said that at any time when he might feel dull, she would be happy to see him; for which he thanked her, with evident gratitude, and said he would willingly profit by her offer.

In this cozy manner the conversation continued for some time, till at last the widow asked him where he intended passing the night. The sacristan was on the point of telling her about the shed, when he remembered she might call upon him there, and discover that he was the owner of the pig, which still kept up his annoyance by incessantly ringing its bell; so he checked himself, and said that it would be on any part of the Common where he could find a dry spot.

" But, my good soul," said the widow, " you will catch your death of cold there, for you are evidently far from strong. I will tell you what I will do. I will make up a little bed for you in the back room."

Before the sacristan could explain how gratefully he accepted her offer, both he and the widow were startled by what at first they considered an unearthly noise, but afterwards found to be the pig howling tremendously, and furiously ringing its bell at the same time.

"Somebody must surely be killing that pig," said the widow.

" Poor pig!" said the sacristan, with great resignation in his tone; "it is very sad, but we should remember it is the lot of its race, and we ought to smother our feelings."

The widow now left the room to prepare the bed, and in a few minutes again entered, saying that all was ready.

Terrible as had been the cries of the pig before, they were *sotto voce* compared with those it now uttered. They might with ease have been heard as far as Newington; and to add to the discomfort, the sacristan could easily perceive that they were gathering a crowd about the house. What to do he knew not. He was perfectly aware the pig would not cease its annoyance so long as he remained in the house, and he had not the heart to leave, he was so comfortable in it. He endeavoured to support the infliction for nearly an hour longer, when, fearing that the widow would feel irritated if the pig continued its cries, and as he particularly wished to stand well in her good graces, he told her that happy as he was it was hardly becoming an anchorite to indulge in so much luxury, and that with much genuine sorrow he must leave her. She attempted to dissuade him, but in vain; and, with a profusion of thanks for her kindness, he left the house.

He found in the road not only the pig, which was now silent, but a great crowd as well. He pushed

through them and was soon lost to their sight in
the darkness. He had hardly proceeded a hundred
yards when the pig joined him. The sight of the
poor animal put him into a great passion, and as a
reward for its ill-timed services, he bestowed on its
ribs a dozen hearty kicks, resolving in his mind that
if he were acting wrongly he would repent of it
afterwards.

When he arrived at the shed he went to his corner,
and first took down his bottle of wine, which he placed
by his side. He passed a large portion of the night
in meditation, principally on the good qualities of the
widow, with occasional thoughts on the pig. From
time to time he put the bottle to his lips and took

a hearty draught to keep the warmth of his person up
to the same temperature as it would have reached on
an African desert.

When day broke he found the imp in the shed,
accompanied by two others, more hideous than
himself.

"You passed a very respectable night for an
anchorite," said one.

" In what was I at fault ? "

" Your treatment of your friend the pig was infamous. You know you do not love him."

" I admit it," said the sacristan. " As an anchorite it is my duty to detach myself from earthly affections, and the pig is a mundane animal."

" So is the widow," said the imp.

" But the widow has a soul," said the sacristan, " and it is my duty to talk seriously to her."

. " And a pretty face, and money as well," said the imp.

" You may attempt to disturb my meditations by talking of the widow and her attractions as much as you please," said the sacristan, " but you will not annoy me."

" Of that I am perfectly persuaded," said the imp; " but we will talk of something else. How do you intend occupying yourself to-day ? "

" I have to go to the City for some more wine."

" Very like an anchorite, indeed," said the imp, reversing the empty bottle, from which but one drop fell.

" If you can prove to me that the anchorites of old would not have done the same during a cold night on Kennington Common, I will leave it off; till then I shall continue it."

So saying, he put on his cap and left the shed, the pig making no attempt to follow him.

The sacristan continued this method of life for two or three days longer. During the time he made several

attempts to call on the widow, but each time the
pig kept so close to his heels that he was obliged to
desist.    One calm moonlight night he thought he
would take a walk.    He strolled in the direction of
Camberwell, the pig following him.    Presently he
saw two female figures a little in advance, and he
hastened to overtake them.    When he had reached

them he found they were
dressed like ladies, but
so muffled up in coifs
and cloaks that it was
impossible for him to
see whether they were
young or old, handsome
or ugly.    He entered
into conversation with
them, and they answered
him  very  courteously.
He walked by their side, talking of the beauty of the
night and other congenial subjects.    They continued
walking on, conversing very discreetly, the pig from
time to time ringing its bell, not in an angry manner,
but simply as if in doubt on some subject passing
in its mind.    They proceeded with their walk till it
got very late, and the heavens became covered with
thick clouds, which totally obscured the moon from
their sight.

At last, when it was at least ten o'clock, the sacristan was on the point of stopping to wish his fair
companions good night, as it was time for him to

return, when they heard before them the sounds of a
violin most exquisitely played, but they could not see
the performer. They continued their road onwards,
listening to the music (by-the-bye it was the same
air the devil played to Tartini in his sleep some
hundred years afterwards). A spell seemed to be
on them, for they could not stop, but followed the
invisible musician. The pig now began to be very
uneasy, and rang its bell in an angry manner; the
sacristan, however, paid no attention to it, but
walked onwards.

In this manner they marched for at least two
hours, when at last the sacristan found himself on
the borders of Blackheath. One of his lady companions then said to him, " We are going to a very
pleasant party to-night a little way farther on. I wish
you would accompany us; I am sure you would be
well received, and you would have an opportunity of
immensely improving the minds of the company."

In spite of the anger of the pig the sacristan consented, and presently they found themselves in the
midst of a circle brilliantly lit up. On one side was
a raised orchestra for some musicians, all of whom
were of the most extraordinary shapes with instruments as strange. Their music, however, was of the
most delightful description, so much so as to dispel
all fear on the part of the sacristan, and inspire him
with a wish to dance. Presently the whole circle
was filled with dancers, all of the most fantastic,
and many even of the most horrible shapes; still

he felt no ear, but stood aside wishing to join them. At last his two lady companions, who had been standing beside him, threw off their wrappers, and appeared in costumes so disgracefully *décolleté*, that the author declines to describe them. The ladies seized the sacristan each by a hand and drew him gently into the middle of the circle, and then commenced dancing. The orchestra at the time played more brilliantly than ever, while the poor pig ran round and round outside the circle, uttering the most discordant sounds and ringing its bell furiously. The sacristan now danced with all

his might, his grotesque figure flying about in all directions, while he performed the most eccentric steps. He became more and more excited with the scene, and danced with still greater vigour. But in a moment the whole vanished, and he found himself in pitchy darkness in the midst of the heath, and in a pouring shower of rain. He listened for a moment for the bell of his pig, but it was no longer heard. The spell under which he had been labouring for some days past was broken, and he found he had been making a great fool of himself. With much difficulty he discovered the high road to London, and arrived at his lodgings about daybreak. The next morning he commenced a new life. He became, not superciliously pious, but a good charitable man, doing his duty in the church, giving alms of all he had to the poor, and contented with being thought no better than his neighbours.

# VI.

## THE RING OF FRASTRADA.

The Governor of Windsor Castle received Master Walter most courteously, and paid him every attention in his power. During the week the merchant remained with him, the Governor almost daily accompanied him in the chase, and many a brave stag fell beneath their cross-bow bolts. Master Walter, in his youth, had been brought up in the country, and although his present avocations were naturally antagonistic to field sports, he had retained his fondness for them, and used to narrate with great unction to his fellow-citizens at their banquets the feats he had accomplished when a young man. It would naturally have been imagined that Master Walter's skill would have fallen off from disuse, but that appeared by no means to be the case. On the contrary, the head verderer of the forest said he had not only never seen a more skilful shot, but had rarely met with a man, (not a genuine forester,) who was better acquainted with the mysteries of the chase or the peculiarities in the flight and stratagems of the stag.

Master Walter himself was astonished at his prowess, but felt no pleasure in it. For the first day or two the change of air seemed to have a beneficial effect on his health, but it soon again relapsed; he went to the chase whenever the weather allowed him, but the exercise at last fatigued him greatly. The pains in his head continued undiminished, his appetite indifferent, and his apathy to every occurrence very great.

As the week drew to a conclusion Bertha, who, to do her justice, had been unremitting in her attention to her father, now began anxiously to wish the week was ended that she might return to London. There would then remain but one week before the Court ball, and the reader, however indifferent to 'ladies' dress, must admit that seven days are barely sufficient for a young girl to make preparations for an affair of the kind. Bertha was of that opinion, and she saw with pleasure a week after their arrival at Windsor the saddle and pack horses in the court-yard, which were to convey herself and her father to London. With ill-simulated regret on her part, and almost apathy on that of her father, they took leave of the courteous Governor, and in the evening of the same day arrived in London.

The day after their arrival in London, Doctor Ambrose, the King's leech, called on Master Walter. With professional gravity he questioned him on his symptoms, and seemed to reflect deeply on his answers. It was evidently a most obscure case, one in fact he had

never before met with in the course of his extensive
practice.    Although he evidently placed little faith
in Master Walter's statement that his brain was
made of glass, he was obliged to admit there was
considerable excuse for the notion.    The dead weight
he felt in his head, the clear-sightedness which
attended all his operations, the apathy he felt on all
subjects in which prior to his malady he would have
felt great interest, the sensation of inorganic coldness he experienced, all seemed to justify the suspicion.    What to do or what to prescribe fairly
puzzled the worthy doctor, as well as annoyed him,
for he felt a great respect for Master Walter, and
sincerely wished to benefit him if he could.    He,
however, suggested a certain course for his patient
to follow, and then he turned to Bertha and asked·
her what preparations she was making for the Court
ball.

Bertha, in her turn, entered with much readiness
into the question, dilating with great satisfaction on
the various arrangements she was making for her
dress, which was to be one of the most magnificent
ever seen in England, but which we will not here
stop to describe, as we shall have a better opportunity on the night of the ball itself.

"You must make great haste, doctor," she said,
" and get my father well, as I cannot go to the ball
without his protection ; besides, I should not enjoy
myself for one moment if I knew he was suffering
at home."

"My dear child," said the physician, "better or worse your father will have my direct prohibition against leaving the house on the night of the King's ball."

Bertha said nothing, but the expression of her countenance told her chagrin.

"My dear," said her father, "my remaining at home shall not disappoint you. I will make such arrangements as will allow you to go."

"But, father, the knowledge that you are kept at home by illness will deprive me of all pleasure. I will not go if you do not."

"There you are very wrong," said the physician. "If your father's health should be improving at the time, as I trust it will be, the certainty of it ought to increase your pleasure, and the knowledge that you are enjoying yourself will, I am sure, be a source of great satisfaction to him. If he should be worse I will not deny that you will be perfectly justified in remaining at home."

"You wish to please me," said Bertha, "and therefore speak as you do. I am sure if you were in my place you would remain at home."

"I will prove to you," said the doctor, "that you are in error. My dear wife has been far from well for the last two or three days. Should she be better on the night of the ball, though not well enough to accompany me, I shall certainly go. I have, it is true, but little pleasure in amusements of the kind, but I shall attend the ball if only to show my respect for his Majesty's invitation."

"There will be no occasion for your remaining at home, Bertha," said Master Walter. "You can do me no good, and, as the doctor says, it will give me great pleasure to know that you are being amused."

"But, father," said Bertha, "it is impossible that I can go without some protection."

"That I admit," said Master Walter, "but I will tell you how it may be arranged. The Lord Mayor and his wife and sister are going, and I will request them to take you; consequently, the question of protection is settled."

"So far as the Lord Mayor and his wife are concerned," said Bertha, "I should not have the slightest objection to go with them; but his sister is my abhorrence. She is so conceited and ridiculous, and so proud of her brother being Lord Mayor, that everybody laughs at her."

"Never mind, my dear," said her father, "no one will laugh at you, depend upon it."

The conversation continued for some minutes longer in the same strain, and at last it was determined that Bertha should go to the ball under the protection of the Lord Mayor, and his wife and sister.

There was nothing particularly worthy of notice till the day of the ball, with the exception that Master Walter's health did not improve. It is more than likely that he was worse, but he concealed it from his daughter that he might not mar the pleasure of her evening.

Early in the afternoon Bertha commenced laying out in her chamber her dress and ornaments for the ball. In this she was assisted not only by her waiting-maid, but by a young lady friend who, though not invited to the ball, had a great wish to see some of its splendour. This young lady had been some years in Cologne, and had but lately returned to England. While they were chatting on different subjects, now on the ball, now on the adventures of the young lady in Germany, to their great disgust Dame Gertrude, the Lord Mayor's sister, was announced. She was an elderly, wealthy widow, very ugly, and intensely conceited. She imagined every fine gentleman that paid her the slightest atten-  tion was in love with her. The two friends, much as they disliked Dame Gertrude, received her with much courtesy, and she entered into their conversation.

"My friend Margaret was telling me as you entered, Dame Gertrude," said Bertha, "a story of a wonderful ring possessed by the Queen Frastrada, the wife of Charlemagne. Any one having it about them could make the individual they admired fall deeply in love with them as long as they held it. She led poor Charlemagne a terrible life with it they say, for he disliked the sight of any other woman. She was punished for her tyranny, however, for an old Bishop obtained possession of it, and wished Frastrada to fall in love with him, which she did, a circumstance which so enraged the King, that he determined on killing the Bishop, who, to cure Frastrada of her love, threw the ring away. Margaret was saying she wished she had found it."

"I said nothing of the kind," said Margaret. "If a man would not love me without a spell of the kind, he might keep his love to himself."

The widow said nothing at the time, but, as she greatly admired a handsome nobleman in attendance on the King who would not even look at her in return, it is more than probable she wished she had it in her possession.

Dame Gertrude now spoke of the object of her visit. It was to inform Bertha that she would meet her at the ball, as she could not go with her brother, the Lord Mayor, as they were not living in the same house, but that he would call for her (Bertha) in good time.

"By-the-bye, my dear," she said, "you have never yet shown me your beautiful mirror, of which I have heard so much; would you let me see it before I go?"

"Certainly," said Bertha; and the three immediately left the room for the chamber in which the mirror was. Dame Gertrude was in ecstacies when she saw it.

"Oh, how lovely!" she exclaimed; "I never saw anything half so beautiful. Why, I declare one looks handsomer in it than one really is. Do you not think so, dear?"

"I am not quite sure of that," said Bertha, who had no indifferent opinion of her own charms.

"I agree with you," said Margaret to Dame Gertrude. "If we could always look as well as the mirror paints us, we need not wish for the ring of Frastrada."

"I wish I had it, nevertheless," thought the widow; but she said nothing.

After a few more expressions of admiration on the beauty of the mirror, Dame Gertrude took her leave.

Dame Gertrude on her road home amused herself in thinking over the arrangement of her toilette for the night, and speculating on the effect she was likely to produce. She drew pictures of the attentions which would be offered her, and anticipated the pleasure she should receive in the different dances, and was not altogether insensible to the charms of the supper. Arrived at her own house she found lying on the stairs, as the door was opened, an old battered-looking ring, apparently of some coarse metal. She had in fact trod on it, and it had caused her considerable pain, and her anger was immediately

roused.   She scolded her servant well for her carelessness in allowing a thing of the sort to remain
on the step, and then turning round she threw it
into the street, and it was instantly picked up by
a sturdy rough-looking mendicant, who placed it in
his wallet.

"May the blessing of all the saints rest on you,

my noble lady," he said, addressing Dame Gertrude in a
whining tone.  "Pray bestow
your charity on a poor man
who has already walked fifty
miles to-day without breaking
his fast."

"The charity I would give
you," said Dame Gertrude,
"and all lazy vagabonds like
you, is the stocks. Take yourself off this moment, or I will
send for the parish constable, and he will give you a
lesson you will not readily forget."

"I wish you were my sweetheart for the next
four-and-twenty hours," said the man to himself as
he turned round to go away, "and it would go hard
with me if I did not teach you a little civility."

"Stay, my poor man," said Dame Gertrude, with
an extraordinary change in her tone and manner;
"stay.  You appear tired and hungry.  Come in,
and I will give you something to eat."

The vagabond could hardly believe his ears,

but he nevertheless turned round and entered the house.

"Martha," said Dame Gertrude, addressing her old servant, "bring up the cold pheasant and some wine, and place them in my sitting-room."

Martha looked astonished, but did not move. She thought it was some plan of her mistress to get the man to the house, and then to send for the constable.

"Do you hear what I say," said Dame Gertrude, getting into a towering passion, "or are you deaf as well as stupid? Get the pheasant immediately, or you will get your ears soundly boxed, I can tell you."

Martha, thus conjured, left the room to fetch the delicacies, wondering to herself what could have come over her mistress, the exercise of charity being one of the least of Dame Gertrude's virtues.

"Do not be angry with the lazy creature," said Dame Gertrude to the beggar, "for if you are I will turn her away, although I could hardly do without her, as she knows my ways well."

"I should be very sorry if you turned her away," said the beggar, "on my account, at any rate till after dinner."

"Sit down," said Dame Gertrude; "you must be sorely tired after your long walk."

"Thank you, my lady, I am."

"Those clothes of yours," said Dame Gertrude, "are very worn and old; come here to-morrow and I will get you some new ones. You shall be dressed like a gentleman."

"I am very much obliged to your ladyship," said the beggar. "I am sure good clothes will become me, although I never tried them."

Martha now entered the room with the pheasant and the wine, and placed them before the beggar,

who immediately attacked them in a very voracious manner, drinking the wine in such large draughts, that Dame Gertrude became somewhat alarmed lest he should make himself tipsy. When he had finished he rose to leave, and made her a speech in the true mendicant whine, thanking her for her charity and promising her the blessing of all the saints in Paradise. She appeared greatly moved at his gratitude, and wished him good night, bidding him call again on her on the morrow, and she followed him with loving eyes as he left the house.

Directly after his departure, she remembered it was possible that he had no money with him, and she therefore put on her coif and left the house to give him some. When in the street she found he was already out of sight, and she asked several of the passers-by if they had seen him? At last one said he had seen a sturdy vagabond who somewhat resembled the description going down one of the streets leading to Wapping. "The rascal," he continued, "seemed half drunk; I sincerely wish a constable would meet him and lock him up in the cage all night to sober him."

Dame Gertrude could hardly contain her anger at hearing such a description of the man she admired, and was on the point of explaining herself somewhat explicitly on the subject, when the thought struck her that it would be better to follow the mendicant immediately, as she probably would not be able to find him. She now started off at a run down Eastcheap. It had begun to rain violently and the streets were ankle-deep in mud; she however took no notice of these inconveniences, but kept on her course. The rain continuing, her clothes at last became thoroughly saturated and clung to her person, and this, together with the mud with which she was splashed, had altered her appearance to such a degree, that any one would rather have taken her for a dirty slattern than the neat cleanly woman she really was.

Onward she went, but she could see nothing of the mendicant, her love for him increasing with her disappointment. She made several inquiries of people she met, but as now there was not a particle of the lady in her appearance, she not unfrequently got very rude answers. She however was not discouraged, but kept on her way till she had arrived at Tower Hill. She crossed it and entered the mass of low dens which surrounded St. Catherine's Hospital, on the spot where the Docks now stand. On passing a collection of disreputable looking houses, she heard sounds of great jollity issuing from one

of the largest. As it was now getting dark and she could not be seen, she approached, and looking through the half-opened door she perceived a number of beggars and women assembled together round a fire in the centre, the smoke escaping by a hole in the roof. The party were engaged in drinking from a leathern mug, which they handed from one to the other, and many of them appeared already quite intoxicated. All the drinkers were seated on the ground with the exception of one, who had placed himself on an empty tub from which he was addressing the others. He appeared to be king of the party, and although three-parts intoxicated himself, he contrived to maintain some semblance of order among the rest. In this man Dame Gertrude recognised the individual with whom she had fallen so deeply in love.

What to do at the moment she knew not. A certain attraction appeared to draw her forward, while the natural feelings of a lady seemed to withhold her. At last doubting was no longer of use, for some one caught her round the waist and dragged her into the hovel, exclaiming at the same time, "A recruit, a recruit. Brothers and sisters, I bring you a recruit for our band."

All looked round with astonishment at Dame Gertrude, who bashfully held down her head. Presently the vagabond, holding in his possession the ring of Frastrada, recognised her, and, making use of a most hideous oath, leaped from the tub to receive her.

"My beauty," he said, taking her hand, "come here, and let me show you to our friends. This is the darling," he continued, "who feasted me so nobly to-day. Receive her, brothers and sisters, with cheers." A loud shout of welcome arose from the meeting, which Dame Gertrude with courtesy, but evident disgust on her countenance, gracefully acknowledged.

"She seems a precious proud one," said one beggar to another.

"No matter," said the other. "If she will find us in drink she may be as proud as she pleases."

Dame Gertrude's lover now made room for her on the floor beside him, and presenting the leathern mug to her, he insisted on her drinking to the health of the gang. She endeavoured to excuse herself, but in vain; so, closing her eyes and holding her breath, she drank to the health of the meeting.

"That's a good wench," said her lover, passing

his arm round her waist and giving her a hearty kiss. "That's a good girl; we shall do very well, I see; but you must remember I am king here, and no one is allowed to disobey me. Now, as we have no more to drink, I propose that my Queen here stand treat and send for some."

Dame Gertrude whispered to her lover, imploring him not to let them drink any more, as they had already had quite enough. He, however, would not listen to reason, but insisted on her advancing the money. She did this, at last, unwillingly enough placing a crown piece in his hand, which was immediately given to one of the party, who was then dispatched to the nearest tavern to fetch wine. During his absence Dame Gertrude endeavoured to examine the friends and acquaintances of the man of her choice somewhat more minutely than she had hitherto done. They consisted of beggars of the district, some of them of the most hideous description, the women, if possible, worse than the men. Many of them were very much deformed, but, such was their depraved appearance, they excited not the slightest pity in her mind. Others had taken off the sham blood-stained bandages which had bound their limbs in the morning. The false blind now saw perfectly well, and the dumb spoke with great fluency, and in a language which, infatuated as she was with her love for their king, filled her with disgust and abhorrence.

The man who had been sent for the wine now

returned, and they again began drinking. The wine acted with marvellous effect upon them, and in a short time many appeared mad drunk. The most reasonable sang or rather roared out ribald songs, and the whole den became a scene of the most horrible confusion and riot. Even the king felt its influence, and conducted himself, if possible, more obstreperously than his subjects. At last, noticing that Dame Gertrude did not drink, he insisted on her doing justice, as he called it, to her own wine, and offered her the leathern tankard. She declined it, pushing the tankard away from her lips when he offered it to her. The king, without speaking, rose from his seat, and taking from the wall a crutch, which one of the false lame, now no longer requiring it, had placed there, he held it over her head in a threatening manner, and the unhappy woman, to pacify him, took the nauseous cup from the ground and attempted to drink, but was unable, so strong was the disgust it excited in her. Fortunately her

lover did not notice the expression of abhorrence on her face, nor the fact that she had not drunk; so he again seated himself by her side and kissed her. She took his hand in hers, and rewarded him with a look of love and gratitude which, however, was quite lost on him.

Although the men seemed satisfied with her presence among them, many of the women showed signs of great discontent, being jealous of the attention the king of the beggars paid to her; and the wine they had drunk so far deadened their prudence that they began to speak of her without any reservation or disguise.

They were led by a powerful virago who had hitherto enjoyed the especial attention of his majesty.

"Madam," she said, "thinks herself much above us, no doubt; but I will bring her dainty airs down for her before long, or my name is not Alce."

"Serve her right, too," said another, "and you shall have my help if you want any."

"Want help against such a thing as that!" said the first speaker. "I should be ashamed of myself if I were not a match for a dozen such as she is."

"Ladies," said the king, taking up the crutch which he had laid beside him, and holding it as a sceptre, "let me advise you to moderate your language, or I shall be obliged to interfere."

" I shan't hold my tongue for you or anybody," said the fury who had first spoken ; "and if you talk to me any more I will set my nails into your beauty's face at once."

" Don't," said the king, holding up the crutch.

The other men now interfered, and peace for the moment was partially restored.

" I must say," said a brawny beggar, " that this ain't fair treatment for Alce. She ought not to be set down in that manner."

The little restraint his majesty had hitherto placed upon himself now vanished, and seizing the crutch he dealt his rebellious subject such a tremendous blow on the skull that it felled him as a butcher would knock down an ox.

Now it happened that the victim was a great favourite among the gang, both male and female, and several rose to take his part. A terrible riot ensued, and blows were dealt freely from all sides among the men, while the women screamed lustily. It happened, however, that a strong party of the watch were at that moment passing, and hearing the noise they entered. So furious, however, was the strife, that the combatants paid no attention to the presence of the watch, and it was only by a free use of the halberds that anything like order was restored.

" So here I have got you at last," said the head constable. " I have long been wanting to find some of you. Seize that fellow," he said, pointing to the king, "and that jade by his side; and you, mistress," he said, perceiving Alce, " I must trouble you to come also, as we want to say something very particular to you. And you others, let me advise you to stop your quarrel, else I shall be obliged to take a few more of you as well; and if I do your shoulders shall smart for it, I can tell you."

The constables now took with them Dame Gertrude, the king of the beggars, and the virago. When outside the hovel the chief constable told off two of his men to take them to the cage, and the culprits were marched off accordingly. When they had got some distance, the king said softly to Dame Gertrude,

" If you have got any money with you let me have it, and I will soon get free from these fellows."

Dame Gertrude without hesitation placed all she had, three crowns, in his hands.

"Can't this affair be smoothed over?" said the king to one of the constables. "If it can, and you shall let us go, I will give you three crowns."

" No, thank you, "said the constable, " your credit is bad."

" I will pay you on the nail," said the beggar.

" I don't know what my mate would say to it," said the constable, " but I will ask him."

The first constable drew the other aside and told him of the offer, and in a little time it was agreed that the prisoners should lag behind, and then choosing their opportunity decamp. The mendicant then placed the three crowns in the hands of the constable, who immediately advanced with his companion some paces, and directly afterwards the three prisoners started off the contrary way.

While the constables, in the certainty (of course) that their prisoners were following them, were walking quietly towards the cage in Eastcheap, the others were making their way as rapidly as they could to Wapping, nor did they stop till they had arrived at the brick kilns which were then there. The king now advised that they should stop, as they were no longer in danger of pursuit, and it was an excellent place for them to pass the night. All things considered, it would have been difficult for them to find a more eligible place for their bivouac. It was raining heavily, the night was bitterly cold, and from the lateness of the hour (it was now considerably past midnight), it would have been difficult for them to have found any low lodging-house open, even if they had possessed among them sufficient money to pay for the accommodation.

The king at last decided on a spot he considered was well adapted, under their present circumstances, for their night's lodging. It was situated between two brick kilns, and thus they could obtain the shelter of the one to windward, and the warmth from both.

Neither of the ladies offered any objection, and the three seated themselves with their backs against

the warm bricks. Dame Gertrude leant her head
on the shoulder of her lover, who was in a moment
sound asleep and snoring loudly ; the virago on the
other side of him had folded her arms on her breast,

and with her head bent forward was fast dozing off.
After all had been asleep for about an hour, the
king and Dame Gertrude were awakened by a loud
howling, which strongly resembled that of a New-
foundland dog.

They looked round for a moment hardly awake,
when to their surprise they could distinguish mixed
with the howling detached words and sentences.
" You'll break my heart, that you will. O dear !
how wretched I am," and the like. On looking
round they found, to their great astonishment, that
the sounds proceeded from Alce, who had raised her
head and was giving vent to her feelings in this

lugubrious manner. Enraged at being disturbed, the king, after uttering a volley of bad language, requested Alœ, by kicking her, to remove to another spot. The woman arose and seated herself with her back to the opposite brick kiln, and then re-commenced howling louder than before. The king, who had fallen asleep, was again aroused. He ordered her immediately to be silent, or he would take effectual means to make her quiet. Alœ made no answer, but continued her howling in a yet louder tone. His majesty now ordered her to leave the place, but no notice was taken of the order. Enraged beyond endurance, he resolved on driving her away, but on trying to rise he found himself stiff and tired and gave up the attempt. But at the same time he was resolved not to be disobeyed, and took up some pieces of brick near him and threw them at her. Some did not hit her but others did, and these last only made her howl the louder without inducing her to leave the spot. His majesty was now almost mad with anger, and threw at her everything he could find near him, even the contents of his wallet. Presently the ring of Frastrada came under his hand, and this also he threw at her, which, after striking her on the head, fell in her lap.

"Oh," she cried out, "how cruelly you treat me, and I who love you so! Do love me again, pray do."

"My precious darling," said the king, rising

from his seat and staggering to her, "and so I do, and I will never again leave you," and throwing himself by her side, he clasped her in his arms.

Dame Gertrude at the moment he threw the ring at the woman, raised her hands to her head, and, pressing them against her brow, remained for some moments in a state of mind similar to a person awaking from a disturbed dream. All her love for the mendicant had vanished, and she felt for him and his companion the most intense abhorrence. Her first idea was to fly, but a moment's reflection showed her how helpless she would be in the hands of the sturdy wretches she was with. When, however, the mendicant rose to soothe the feelings of the virago, she determined on making the attempt to release herself from them. So she quietly rose and ran round to the back of the brick kiln without being perceived. She had now got a fair start, and kept it, running with great celerity till she felt herself secure from pursuit. She now stopped and began to consider which would be her road to London. Fortunately she found herself on the highway, and she followed it and entered the City by Aldgate. Tired, wet, muddy, and footsore, she at last reached home. She had some difficulty in awakening her servant, but at last she succeeded. Happily when Martha opened the door she had no candle in her hand, and thus did not perceive the disordered state of her mistress. She apologised for having no light, and told Dame Gertrude she would

bring her one directly, but she was informed it
would not be required. Dame Gertrude made her
arrangements for the night as she best could in the
dark, and when in bed was soon sound asleep, after
the great fatigue she had experienced during her
night's adventures.

# VII.

## THE PHYSICIAN'S WIFE.

THE Lord Mayor's sister had hardly left the house when Master Ambrose, the King's leech, entered it. He had called to visit his patient, whom he had not seen for four days. When he entered Master Walter's chamber, the merchant had some difficulty in recognising him, his appearance was so much changed since his last visit. The doctor immediately detected the surprise in the mind of his patient.

"You see, Master Walter," he said, "the wreck of the man who called on you a few days since. As you may perceive, grief is strong, and on me it has done its work."

"I am truly sorry," said the merchant, "for the change which has taken place in you, and the more so that grief has occasioned it. Might I ask further information, or should I be acting indiscreetly?"

"When last I saw you," said the doctor, "I told you my poor wife was suffering from a slight indisposition, as I thought. To-day I am a widower. She expired last night, and has left me the most miserable of men. Even now I can hardly realise the extent of my misfortune. I left home this evening to wait on some few of the most urgent of my cases, thinking, perhaps, it would clear my brain, but without effect. I cannot even now, for five minutes together, believe that I have lost her. But let us change the conversation, for I do not wish to sadden you. Are you better?"

"Not in any way," said the merchant, lowering his tone so that Bertha, whose step was heard on the stairs, might not understand him. "The weight in my head is certainly worse than ever."

"I am very sorry to hear it," said the doctor. "It is indeed a most obscure disease: I never in the course of my practice met with one equally so. As soon as this ball is over, on which your daughter appears to have set her heart, I must insist on your leaving town again, and remaining away from business in the country for at least a month or six weeks. The slight sojourn you made at Windsor was not sufficient to give nature a fair trial."

"I will endeavour to do as you wish," said the merchant, "although it will be most inconvenient for me in the present state of my affairs. Never had I more important transactions on hand, or any that required greater care in their completion."

At that moment Bertha entered the room, and the conversation on the subject of the merchant's health dropped. At a glance, Bertha saw that some misfortune had befallen the doctor, but she hardly liked to make any inquiry as to its nature; her father, however, informed her.

" Bertha, my dear," he said, " a dreadful calamity has fallen on our dear friend the doctor. His wife, of whom you have so often heard him speak, is no more."

Bertha was silent with astonishment.

" Do not speak to me, my dear, on the subject," said Master Ambrose. " I know you wish to do so, but it will be painful to you, and immeasurably more so to myself." Then changing the subject, he continued : " I have been talking to your father on the state of his health. I told him that as soon as this ball is over, I will insist upon his again going into the country, and remaining there at least a month or six weeks; but he appears to think it will be inconvenient, although he is willing to obey me. Now I must get you to assist me. Promise me you will go with him, and not allow him to talk, and if possible not to think of business during the whole of the time. I assure you it is highly necessary, else he will suffer for it."

" You may depend upon me," said Bertha, " I will do everything in my power to make him obey your instructions."

The doctor now took leave of Master Walter, and Bertha accompanied him out of the room. She wished to have a little conversation with him alone on the subject of her father's health, and for that purpose conducted him into the mirror chamber.

She here conversed with him for some time, listening to his description of her father's malady, and inquiring carefully into the course the doctor would advise her to follow in nursing the invalid. As Master Ambrose was on the point of leaving the room his eye caught the mirror.

"And this," said he, "is the beautiful glass of which my poor wife spoke so highly. Alas! everything I see to-night reminds me that I have lost her for ever. Oh, my dear wife," he said, the tears running down his face the while, "willingly would I give a year of my existence if I could but reanimate your corpse for one whole day!"

Here his sorrow became so profound that Bertha, selfish as she naturally was, wept from pure sympathy. The doctor at last saw her tears.

"My dear child," he said, "excuse me. I would not willingly make you sad at any time, less than all at a moment like this, when you are promising yourself so much pleasure. Good night, and do not forget my instructions respecting your father."

We will leave Master Ambrose to visit some of his most urgent cases, while we shortly recount the story of his life.

Master Ambrose was the son of very poor but honest parents, who, without being able to give him any education, brought him up both by precept and practice piously and honestly. From his constant attendance at the parish church he came under the notice of the priest, who occasionally employed him

to assist in the mass.    Finding the lad had considerable natural abilities, the worthy priest, with the
tact habitual to the Catholic priesthood, took great
pains in giving him the rudiments of a good education, intending to bring him up for the church.    The
boy was diligent, respectful, and attentive, and profited so much by the kindness shown him, that it
would have been difficult to have found a lad of
seventeen years of age better instructed.    By this
time he had lost both his parents, and the good
priest, who had first noticed him, died shortly afterwards.    His successor, however, likewise took a
great interest in the boy, and continued to him the
same protection as his predecessor.    Everything
seemed to promise that young Ambrose would one day
become a shining light in the ecclesiastical profession;
and all the clergy showed him great favour.    Among
those who took the greatest interest in him was a
certain Father Theodore, a monk who was reckoned
one of the most learned leeches in England; for
in those days the ecclesiastical bodies held the keys
to all the learned professions.

Young Ambrose for some time acted as the assistant of Father Theodore, who took great pains in
instructing the young fellow in the art of mixing his
medicines, and, what in modern phraseology is
termed, dispensing generally.    In a short time Ambrose became of so much use to the monk, that he
was taken into the convent, a cell allowed him, and his
food given in return for his services in the laboratory.

Four years more passed over Ambrose's head, and he still remained in the monastery, but his duties had undergone a considerable change. He was no longer the laboratory drudge, but the dresser and assistant of Father Theodore. The worthy monk, setting aside all professional jealousy, even frequently requested him to visit his patients for him, and young Ambrose, from his skill, kindness, and humanity, began to make himself much liked by those whom he visited.

The time had now arrived for him to determine whether he would enter the brotherhood, and become one of the order—a decision to which he was greatly encouraged not only by Father Theodore, who was much pleased at the idea of his mantle falling on such worthy shoulders; but by the other monks as well, who looked forward to great honour and profit accruing to their convent by his admission.

After giving the subject his fullest consideration, Ambrose determined on adopting the cowl, and in due course entered on his novitiate. For some months his behaviour gave perfect satisfaction to his superiors. He conducted himself in a pious and regular manner, and gave his unremitting attention, not only to the rich patients, who made liberal offerings to his order, but to the sick poor as well, so that there was every prospect of his becoming one of the most esteemed as well as one of the most celebrated leeches in the metropolis.

At last, however, a singular change came over

him. From being good-humoured and energetic,
he became sad and unhappy, and this was the
more extraordinary as there did not appear the
slightest reason for the change. Nothing had happened to displease him, and all the monks showed
him the kindest feeling, yet he avoided their society,
and was, when not engaged in the active duties
of his profession, silent and reserved. At last the
secret came out—Ambrose had fallen desperately in
love with the only daughter of one of his patients,
an aged woman, very poor, but of highly respectable
family. Eleanor de Rodon, the daughter, was a
beautiful girl, of about nineteen years of age, and as
good as she was lovely. The novice had to call frequently on the mother, and each time the daughter
saw him. Very soon the mother had to notice in
the daughter's conduct a change somewhat similar to that remarked by the monks in Ambrose.
Perhaps of the two the change was in her the
greater, for not only did she try to conceal her
love, but the fear was over her that her attachment, if not criminal, had a certain shade of the
impious in it, as Ambrose was, if not absolutely,
at least in intention, a member of one of the holy
bodies.

The love of the young people for each other increased with every visit of Ambrose to the house.
She admired him the more each time she saw
him, while he, from noticing the devoted attention
the girl paid her sick mother, became daily more

enamoured of her, without one word of love having
passed between them.

The mother died and was buried. Ambrose at
first resolved that he would abstain from visiting at
the house, but the helpless state of Eleanor, and her
profound grief for her mother, so preyed upon him
that he relinquished his resolve and endeavoured to
console her to the best of his power. The result
may easily be anticipated. The couple discovered,
what they might have known before, that they were
desperately in love with each other, and they determined, as soon as the time of Eleanor's mourning
for her mother was over, to marry. It is true,
Eleanor made many objections at first, and intimated
many scruples in consequence of Ambrose's intention
to enter holy orders; but he proved to her so
logically, that during his novitiate he was at liberty
at any time to quit the clerical profession, love
rendering her so much aid in understanding his
arguments, that at last, without further hesitation,
she accepted the offer of his hand.

Now came a terrible trial for Ambrose,—the duty
of informing the superior of his determination to
leave the monastic life, and to continue his profession as a civilian. Day after day he delayed the
confession, but at last his courage, or rather his
love, supported him, and in full conclave he informed
the brethren of the order of his intention to marry.
Had a thunderbolt fallen suddenly amidst them they
could not have been more startled than they were at

the information. For some time they sat dumb with surprise, as they could hardly believe the intelligence, and it was only when Ambrose repeated his statement that they fully comprehended him.

It was indeed a terrible shock to the reverend body, for Ambrose was, of all the novices they had, the one of greatest promise. The monks then endeavoured by persuasions and arguments to make him forego his resolution. They told him of the bliss which would await him hereafter if he kept true to the church. They reminded him of the friendship, respect, and esteem they held him in. They endeavoured to arouse his ambition by pointing out to him the possibility that many years hence he might be chosen, from his abilities and piety, the superior of the order, but all in vain. The blind god was more powerful than the whole body of monks together, and Ambrose kept true to Eleanor.

The brethren of the order, however, were resolved not to give up their hold on Ambrose as long as there was the shadow of probability that they might retain him. They met in solemn conclave to deliberate on the matter. One of the brethren, perhaps the most bigoted of the whole, inquired who might be the young woman who had ensnared Ambrose, and was told it was a very beautiful girl, the daughter of a respectable widow who had been Ambrose's patient.

The monk who had asked the question now rose from his seat, and with great gravity addressed the others. He reminded them how strongly attached Ambrose had hitherto been to the interests of the order, and how resigned to the lot in life which he had carved out for himself.

Had he been of a flighty or restless disposition, idle or indisposed to learn, or negligent of his religious duties, his leaving the service of the church would have been little to be wondered at; but a young man whose life was so irreproachable as that of

Ambrose, was not likely to quit the career he had entered upon without some great and overpowering cause, and the nature and origin of that cause he considered it the duty of the order to discover. They had been told that the mother of the girl had been a pious, well-disposed woman, but how often was wickedness found under the mask of piety? They were told that the girl herself was a modest, well-disposed girl, but how often was cunning hidden under the mask of simplicity and modesty? How often did the devil assume for the purpose of deceit the form of an angel? In conclusion, he had no hesitation in saying that, all things considered, their dear son Ambrose was at that moment suffering under witchcraft.

The monk sat down, not altogether content with

o 2

the result of his speech, for it received no applause whatever, while Father Theodore, the leech, now old and infirm, expressed his contempt for the arguments used in terms somewhat too strong for a meeting of such reverend men, and thereby drew upon himself a gentle admonition from the prior who presided at the meeting.

Father Theodore then expressed his regret that any hasty expression should have fallen from his lips, but at the same time the arguments of the reverend brother who had spoken before him were certainly of a description to excite his anger. He did not speak out of affection for Ambrose, whom he admitted he loved as a son, but from the interests of human nature and common sense. He reminded the meeting that, good as Ambrose was, he was still mortal and liable to mortal errors. It should also be borne in mind that Ambrose had been thrown far more in the way of temptation from the duties of his medical profession than novices generally were. He also said that he was acquainted both with the girl and her mother. Of the latter he could conscientiously state that she was a pious good woman; of the former he had no hesitation in saying that if he had fifty years less on his head than he had at that moment, and was again a novice, it is more than possible he should relapse with quite as much facility as Ambrose. No one regretted the circumstance more than he (Father Theodore) did, but it was, he feared, too late to remedy it; and he proposed that Ambrose should quit them without anger on their part or annoyance on his.

The speech of Father Theodore carried great weight with it, and the meeting resolved that no obstruction should be thrown in Ambrose's way, and that when he quitted them it should be done in a perfectly friendly manner on all sides.

Ambrose remained within the walls of the monastery not only till the year of his novitiate had ended, but for some time longer, in fact, till the year of Eleanor's mourning had expired. The brethren, finding all opposition to his marriage in vain, treated him with the most thorough good fellowship, with one exception, Father Peter, the monk who had suggested that the girl was a witch. This obstinate bigoted fellow perpetually attacked him on the sin of his contemplated marriage, and endeavoured to prove to him that he was under the influence of magic, offering up prayers in his presence that he might be relieved from the power of Satan, till the very day arrived for Ambrose to leave the brotherhood. He departed with the good feeling of all, except Father Peter, and two days afterwards married Eleanor at the church of St. Mary Axe, taking up his abode in the rooms which had been occupied by his wife and her mother.

As the fortune of Ambrose and his wife, beyond the value of furniture, only amounted to a few crowns, he was of course obliged immediately to commence the practice of his profession to obtain the means of living. As he was not very well known in the locality he resided in, his patients at the commencement were few, but the success of his cures soon brought him fresh practice, and things for some time appeared to promise him ultimate success in his profession, and that too of no second-rate kind.

Suddenly, however, he found himself looked upon with great suspicion, or rather aversion, by several respectable families in the neighbourhood whom he had hoped to have made his friends; and, worse still, his wife appeared to.be even more disliked than himself. He was utterly astonished at the circumstance, at any rate as far as regarded Eleanor, for a more amiable inoffensive woman never lived. In his own case he thought he could partially trace the cause. There resided near him two other practitioners who were ignorant quacks, and these men, he thought, m'ght naturally feel extremely jealous at the presence of a successful new comer.

Still Ambrose worked on, endeavouring by unremitting attention to his patients to neutralize the bad opinion which was evidently abroad in the neighbourhood respecting him. ⌐He did not succeed, however, and one day when he returned to his home, after having experienced some cruel rebuffs in the course of his rounds, he was surprised at not finding his wife there as usual to receive him. He sat himself down for some time waiting her arrival, but as she did not appear he began to be uneasy. He called on a neighbour with whom he was on some slight terms of intimacy, and asked him if he could explain her absence.

" Do you really not know ?" said the neighbour.

" Certainly not ; if you know, pray instruct me, for I am dreadfully anxious about her."

The neighbour looked inquiringly in his face for a few moments, and then said,

" I am sorry to tell you that this morning, shortly after you left the house, she was arrested by a constable at the order of the Bishop, on a charge of witchcraft."

" On a charge of witchcraft !" said Ambrose, astonished. " There must be some mistake in this.

They have arrested her instead of some other person. Oh, this will be easily rectified."

The neighbour said nothing, but from the expression of his countenance Ambrose could easily perceive that he knew more than he chose to say.

" Pray tell me," said Ambrose, now getting greatly alarmed, "if you know anything more. You may imagine the state of mind I am in."

"Well, then, my friend," said the neighbour, "if you do not know I will tell you all, for let your wife be what she will, I believe you are in your heart a humane clever man. There is no mistake, for the warrant, which I saw, is made out clearly enough in her name. The fact is she was suspected of practising magic to seduce you from the cloisters, and of now assisting you in your profession, mixing up witches' nostrums for you to give your patients, whereby you perform wonderful cures to the benefit of their health and the ruin of their souls;" and he concluded by quoting two cases of marvellous cures Ambrose had performed, which the other two leeches, as they were unable to accomplish anything of the kind, said must necessarily have been performed by magic.

Poor Ambrose was now so terrified that he was on the point of fainting, and with great difficulty steadied himself. His astonishment was so great that he could hardly realise his misfortune. Of the two cures mentioned by his neighbour he was not a little proud, and now he found that they were to be brought forward as evidence of the guilt of his wife, and that the assistance she had so kindly rendered him in his little laboratory was also to be used against her.

When he had a little recovered himself, he inquired of his friend if he could inform him to what prison she had been taken, and heard in reply that in consequence of the absence of the Bishop of

London in the country, as well as of the repairs his palace was undergoing, she had been removed to the cells in the palace of the Bishop of Winchester, in Southwark, where he would doubtless hear of her.

Poor Ambrose immediately started off for Southwark and arrived at the palace about nightfall. He there found that the information he had received was perfectly correct, and that Eleanor was confined in one of the cells appropriated for ecclesiastical offenders. He was not allowed to see her, nor could he obtain a word of information about her. All the satisfaction he received was that if he would call again about noon the next day one of the Bishop's chaplains, who had charge of the case, and was commissioned to make inquiries concerning it, would then see him.

With this scant satisfaction he returned to his home and passed the night in fear and sorrow. He knew quite well how easy it was to make accusations of witchcraft and how difficult to disprove them, and how terrible were the punishments in case the prisoner did not succeed in establishing his innocence. Morning at last came and brought with it some slight relief, and also showed him the necessity of thought and prompt action.

Long before noon Ambrose was at the Bishop's palace, and at last was admitted into the presence of the chaplain, whom he found a courteous, amiable man, but evidently much prejudiced against his prisoner. He told Ambrose that the case was a very grave one, and unfortunately from the evidence in his possession he much feared the accusation was true.

Ambrose assured him the accusation was false, that everything he had done, under the blessing of Heaven, was performed by perfectly natural means, and that the two men whom he imagined were her accusers were two ignorant and dishonest quacks.

"I cannot," said the chaplain, "go into the nature of the evidence against her at present, nor say who are her accusers; let it suffice that she shall receive no injustice. On Saturday next call here at mid-day and bring with you what evidence you can to prove the good and pious character of your wife if you are certain the accusation is a false one, as well as proof that the means you used for the cure of the two terrible cases of small-pox were those practised by medical men of learning; and if you can establish those facts depend upon it all will yet end well."

Ambrose thanked him for the information, and requested permission to see his wife, but was told it was impossible under the circumstances, and that he must content himself till the next Saturday, when the chaplain hoped the Bishop would order her release.

In the interim of the three days before the next examination, Ambrose busied himself in collecting evidence for his wife's defence. His first step was to call on the Abbot of the monastery in which he had been a novice, and explain to him the painful

strait he was in. The Abbot listened to him with
great attention and kindness, and promised him all
the help in his power. Still the case appeared a very
serious one. Personally, he said, he knew nothing
of medicine, but he would send for Father Theodore
and consult him on the subject. A messenger
was immediately sent to bring the leech, who
returned with him. Father Theodore was highly

pleased to see his old pupil, and heard with great
indignation the charge which had been brought
against Eleanor.

"I think," said he, "I know who is at the bottom
of this, but it will go hard with me if I do not
conquer the bigoted blockhead yet. Now tell me,
Ambrose, did I rightly understand that the suspicion
that has brought all this terrible misfortune on you
arose from your successful treatment of two cases

of small-pox? If so, tell me what treatment you followed."

Ambrose immediately explained to him what medicines he had used, and what other sanitary courses he had adopted.

The old leech listened attentively, and when Ambrose had finished said, "Why, that is exactly my own treatment."

" Precisely so, father, " said Ambrose; " I followed in these as well as every other case I attend, the lessons I learnt from you."

"Now," said Father Theodore, "who prepared the medicines ? "

"My wife, reverend father, but under my instructions; we are too poor to engage an assistant."

"That," said Father Theodore, " is the most difficult point you will have to work against. Understand me, I perfectly believe all you have said, but unfortunately I am not your judge, else the affair would soon end. Now tell me, has your wife been regularly to mass since you have been married? There will be no difficulty in proving the excellence of her life before it."

" Regularly, reverend father, but not to the parish church of St. Mary Axe, but to St. Mary's-in-the-Spital. The priest of that church has been her confessor ever since her first communion, and was also the confessor of her mother."

" And a very pious, good man he is," said the

Abbot. "I know him well, and would place implicit faith in anything he said."

"I think, my son," said Father Theodore to Ambrose, "you have nothing to fear, but you must not sleep over the affair. Get all the evidence you can, and I on my side will assist you to the best of my abilities, and so I am sure will all our brethren; for, with one exception, you were a favourite with us all."

Ambrose acted fully up to the advice of Father Theodore, and exerted himself most energetically in obtaining evidence, but except in the case of Father Theodore himself, it was all simply for character as to the honourable life and antecedents of the accused.

However, on the point of science Father Theodore was a host in himself, and Ambrose, on the day for the hearing before the Bishop, attended at the palace in the full assurance that his dear Eleanor would soon be liberated.

The cause was heard in the hall of the palace, and the Bishop presided. There were present a considerable body of ecclesiastics of all orders, but no public beyond some witnesses. Many of the monks, as well as the Abbot, were present, and when Ambrose entered the hall, to his great satisfaction he found his friend Father Theodore seated near the Bishop, conversing most familiarly with him; and then Ambrose remembered that the Bishop had been formerly a patient of Father Theodore.

Ambrose waited anxiously and impatiently for the

appearance of his wife, but she·came not. Presently the proceedings were opened, and the Bishop inquired the reason the prisoner was not present, and received for answer that she was too much indisposed to attend; and moreover Father Peter, who had been requested to attend and give evidence, and who in fact was the principal witness against her, was not in attendance. Why, they had not heard.

The Bishop said it would be necessary to postpone the hearing, although he should do so with regret, as it was hardly just either to the prisoner or her husband. He was on the point of arranging with his chaplain on what day next week it would be convenient to hear the case, when Ambrose's friend, the Father Abbot, stood up, and requested to be allowed to make a few remarks.

"I wish," he said, "most respectfully to submit to your Lordship whether there is any real reason for postponing this case. If you would graciously allow me to address you on the subject, I think I could place such facts before you as would prove not only that the prisoner is innocent, but that the accusations which have been brought against her come from those who have acted with prejudice or indecent haste, or from ignorant quacks who have been stimulated by jealousy at the sight of a competitor among them of infinitely greater ability than them-selves."

"I shall be very happy, reverend father, to hear anything you may wish to say," said the Bishop; "I can assure you it will give me great pleasure if you can show me such cause as will allow me to quash the proceedings against this unhappy young woman."

"I am most grateful to your Lordship for your kindness. Not having a copy of the pleadings against her before me, I cannot dispute the accusations seriatim; but I understand one of the gravest is that by magic she seduced the novice Ambrose to quit the cloister and marry her. Into this subject I beg to assure you I went very deeply before the marriage took place, partly stimulated to it by Father Peter, and partly with a wish to retain Ambrose in the cloister if possible, as I considered the addition of so good and learned a young man to our brotherhood would not only be advantageous to us but to the church as well. The result of my inquiries, and those of more than one of our brethren, was, that a more pious, amiable, or excellent young lady it would be difficult to find; and I gave up the question, considering Ambrose's love for the girl to be simply the result of affection. I submit, then, to your Lordship, that in justice that part of the accusation against her should not be heard on the plea of 'autrefois acquit.' My reverend brethren who assisted me in my inquiries are present, and if you please to question them, you will find their decision perfectly corresponds with my own. With respect to her using magical appliances I have no opinion to offer, as I pretend to no medical knowledge; but our brother Theodore here, who you know is a high authority on subjects of the kind, will no doubt give you his opinion on the matter."

"And no better could be given," said the Bishop, smiling graciously on Father Theodore.

"I would submit," said Father Theodore, "before I state my opinion, that the two leeches who I see are now in attendance should first tell us from what circumstances they have come to the conclusion that witchcraft has been used."

"A good suggestion," said the Bishop; "let one of them stand forward and tell us what he knows on the subject."

A bloated, vulgar, commonplace-looking man immediately stepped forward to give his evidence.

"What treatment of Master Ambrose did you notice in the two mysterious cases of small-pox which led you to believe that witchcraft has been practised?" inquired the Bishop.

"Please you, my Lord, I attended one of the cases, and Master Gurdon, who stands behind me, the other. My case I attended with every care, according to the rules of medical science, but it got so bad that I despaired of life, and I thought it my duty to tell the mother that the child could not live. However, I called to see it the next day, when, to my great disgust, I found that the woman the night before had sent for Master Ambrose, who was not known in the district, to attend it. Naturally enough, I said 'Your child may die, then, for I will have nothing more to do with it,' and, in great anger, I left the house. The next week I found that the child had not only recovered so far as to be out of all danger, but that it had been removed to the woman's sister's house, who resides a little way in the country, and that Master Ambrose went every day to see it. I was of course much surprised, and I asked what treatment Master Ambrose had adopted, and I found it had been the reverse of my own, and that he had given it drugs which had been prepared by his wife, and of which I had never before heard. On mentioning the case to Master Gurdon, he told me Ambrose had performed a cure equally great, or greater, on one of *his* patients, and that the medicines had also been made up by the wife. Now, as we had both used the proper remedies for the disease, and as Master Ambrose's treatment had been the reverse of ours, we, of course, thought that improper means had been used in the cures; but still we were averse to taking steps against a brother practitioner until we found that Master Gurdon's cousin's wife had heard from a pious monk, one Father Peter, that he very much suspected a witch had ensnared from his monastery a novice of the name of Ambrose who was skilful in pharmacy, and had married him. We then agreed to call on Father Peter together, and

P

we did so, and explained to him the whole circumstances. He told us it was our duty immediately to inform against her to the priest of the parish church, who directly took up the matter—the more readily as he had never seen Dame Eleanor at the confessional since she had been living in the parish, or even inside the church. . . . . That is all I know of the matter."

"Did you see any of the drugs he made use of?" inquired Father Theodore of the leech.

"I did, reverend Father, and I could not find of what things they were composed, although I studied them carefully."

"Do you happen to have any of them about you?"

"I have, reverend Father;" and he placed on the table a small portion of a drug.

"Now, with the permission of the reverend Bishop, I will ask you to describe your treatment."

"I ordered the windows to be fast closed and the door not to be opened unless to allow some person to enter or leave the room, and that was to be done as quickly and as seldom as possible. I then wrapped the child in a red cloth I always keep for occasions of the kind, very thick and warm, and then covered it well with clothes, and gave it such medicines as I thought would suit it, especially some mummy flesh powdered, of great price."

"Did you ever use that red cloth before, and, if so, with what effect?"

"Sometimes with good effect, considering the deadly nature of the disease."

" And have you used it since ?"

" I have, reverend Father, twice; but in both cases the patient died, which made me more certain than ever that witchcraft had been used."

" Witchcraft or murder!" said Father Theodore, colouring up with passion; "witchcraft or murder, certainly. Now let us see the other doctor, to whose care in Aldgate the lives of his Majesty's lieges are consigned."

Room was instantly made for the other quack to advance, but he did not make his appearance. The fact was he had some knowledge of Father Theodore, if not personally, then by reputation, and he thought it more prudent to avoid the examination. He had left the palace so long before he was called for that he could not be overtaken.

Father Theodore now proposed that Ambrose should be called upon to explain his treatment of the two cases, and his reasons for acting as he had done. This he did so clearly and logically, as to call forth a murmur of approbation from all present, and the compliment of the Bishop, who told him he was evidently a worthy pupil of Father Theodore. Father Theodore now spoke. He said he had examined the drugs before him, and was fully convinced they were of the most simple description, and, in fact, the same as he had used himself in many hundred cases with success— were, in fact, those on which he had advised Ambrose to have special reliance. He called the attention of the Bishop to the practice of the two quacks, who were perfectly justified in saying their patients would certainly have died had they continued their visits, the deaths being caused by the ignorance and malpractice of the medical advisers rather than by the strength of the malady. He concluded by saying with great warmth, that if Ambrose's style of practice was illegal, he himself ought to have been burnt as a wizard fifty times over ; and if causing death by ignorance were murder, no gallows could be found sufficiently high for the two quacks.

The Abbot now spoke. He reminded the Bishop that the behaviour of Dame Eleanor in absenting herself from the service of the church since her marriage had now to be cleared up. But he believed there was a reverend father present who could throw some light on that matter, and he proposed that the priest of St. Mary's-in-the-Spital should be asked to give his evidence. This was readily done. The priest of St. Mary's said that he had known Eleanor since she was a child, and that there was not a member of his flock who had been more piously or correctly educated, and that since her marriage she had been a constant attendant at his church, nor was there one whom he would more readily hold up as an example than her.

The Bishop now inquired if the prisoner had been examined. The chaplain replied "that she had been severely questioned, but that he was obliged to admit that not a word tending to inculpate herself had been extracted from her."

The Bishop now gave his decision. He said with great satisfaction, that he had never heard a case which had terminated in a more honourable manner. He ordered that no further proceedings should be taken in the matter, and that the accused might be liberated immediately.

Ambrose shortly thanked the Abbot and Father Theodore for their kind behaviour, and before the hall was cleared he had left to seek his wife. He was, however, obliged to wait some short time before he could see her,—till the order for her release should be drawn out. He was then conducted to her cell, where he found her stretched on a truckle bed. At first sight he did not notice the deathly pallor of her countenance, as it was now nearly dark, so long time had the pro- ceedings occupied. He flew to her, and

clasped her in his arms, telling her the joyful tidings that she was no longer a prisoner.

Eleanor answered with a voice so low and faint that he could hardly understand her. Presently he found she was too weak to move even on her bed without his assistance; and he then heard that her present condition arose from her having been submitted to the torture.   Ambrose now for the first time understood the answer of the chaplain "that she had been questioned severely."   He burst out into a torrent of grief, accusing the Bishop of cruelty, and was on the point of leaving the cell to upbraid him for his behaviour when the jailer kindly touched him on the arm and showed him the danger both to himself and wife of his acting in such a manner.

The unfortunate man now gave full vent to his grief; clasping his wife round the neck with his arms, and kissing her with the greatest affection. After a few minutes the jailer advised him to obtain a litter to take her home, but the poor fellow had no money with him, and that mode of conveyance was in those days very expensive.   He however told his wife he would leave her for a short time to obtain the money to pay for the litter.   But Eleanor pleaded so earnestly that he should not leave her that he remained for a few minutes longer.

Suddenly she said, "Ambrose, my beloved husband, help me to rise and I will go with you. Heaven, I trust, will give me strength.   If we walk slowly I think I can accomplish it."

Ambrose placed his arms round his wife's waist and assisted her to rise, but notwithstanding all her resolution when she placed her foot on the ground and attempted to walk, she uttered a loud cry of pain which wrung her husband's heart. She seated herself on the bed, and placing her head on her husband's shoulder, remained silent for a few moments, while the tears followed each other down his cheeks, although he attempted to conceal them from his wife by placing his hand across his eyes. When she had rested a few moments she said to him, "I will try again, dear; this time I hope I shall have more courage."

She now slowly rose and stood upon  her foot, her husband the while supporting her with his arm. She uttered no cry, but had it been lighter Ambrose would have perceived from the manner she bit her lip that she was suffering intense pain. Slowly she walked across the cell to the door, and at last, with great difficulty, left the palace.

The couple proceeded for some short distance towards the bridge, but human nature could no longer support the torture, and Eleanor sank fainting on the ground. Her husband, terribly alarmed, raised her and seated her on a door step. Slowly she recovered, but to continue her road was impossible, so Ambrose lifted her in his arms, determining to carry her home. Love gave him strength, and at last he arrived at the foot of the bridge. The ascent was indeed a terrible task for him, he being far from strong, and the crowd he met impeding him greatly. Still he kept on.

The descent on the other side was less fatiguing; but then he had before him the steep acclivity of Fish Street Hill. With immense labour, which nothing but the deepest love could have given him strength and courage enough to support, he arrived at the entrance to Eastcheap. But here again he was obliged to place his wife on a door-step, while he obtained a little rest. After a few minutes he again took her in his arms and continued his road homeward. But when within a few hundred yards of his house his strength gave way, and he sank with his burden on the ground.

A crowd now collected round him, and he, much annoyed at their remarks, again attempted to raise his wife, but it was useless. All strength had left him.

" Will no good Christian help me ? " he said. " I fear my wife is dying, and I have but a short distance to reach my home."

A good-natured powerful man stepped forward, and was on the point of taking Eleanor in his arms, when a woman said to him, " Leave her alone: don't you see it is the doctor's witch-wife ? Leave her alone, or you will come to harm."

The man immediately refused to assist her, and Ambrose, making a desperate effort, raised her from the ground, and staggering the while again proceeded towards his home, followed by a crowd calling out

all the way, "There goes the doctor's witch-wife!
There goes the doctor's witch-wife!" These taunts
seemed to give fresh strength to Ambrose, until at
last he arrived at home, and placed his wife on the
bed. He then fell on the floor helpless and senseless
from fatigue.

Next morning Ambrose had somewhat recovered
from his great exertions, but poor Eleanor remained in a deplorably weak condition. Ambrose
now busied himself in making preparations for the
future. After having assisted his wife he left his
home to seek for a nurse, and went to two or
three houses where he thought he would be able to
find a woman for the purpose. In vain, no one
would attend on her. Her reputation as a witch
had been spread all over the neighbourhood, through
the instrumentality of the two quacks, and neither
prayers, entreaties, nor the promise of a double reward, succeeded in removing the prejudices of these
ignorant women. In his despair he applied to the
neighbour who had informed him of the imprison-
ment of his wife, and requested his advice. He told
all that had taken place, how the Abbot of the
monastery in Bermondsey as well as the monks
had attended, and not only proved the excellent
reputation of Eleanor before her marriage, but also
that the system he had adopted in the cure of the
two cases of small pox had been perfectly scientific
and natural. He also mentioned the evidence of the
parish priest of St. Mary's-in-the-Spital, who showed

the excellence of her married life.  He told him, too, that Eleanor had been subjected to the torture without a word which could tend to her prejudice being elicited from her, and that now she was suffering terribly from the effects of it, yet no one could be found who would attend her as a nurse.

The neighbour listened to his recital both with patience and sympathy, but told him he did not know how he could assist him in the matter, or he would have done so willingly.  He reminded him how difficult it was to eradicate a prejudice of the kind from the minds of the ignorant vulgar, and he advised Ambrose to attend to his wife himself, and give up the thought of establishing himself in practice in that neighbourhood.  "If I were you," he said, "I would try some other locality, where your wife is not known. If you remain here you will be perpetually annoyed, and with your ability you would have but little difficulty in finding patients anywhere.  Take courage, and do not allow yourself to be cast down, and all will yet end well, depend upon it."

Ambrose left him, determined to follow his advice. When he arrived at home he found Eleanor somewhat easier, but still so weak that he would not allow her to talk.  He seated himself by her bedside, and reflected on his prospects for the future.  They seemed very dark indeed, for although he possessed energy, ability, and courage, he was very poor, and the expenses attendant on Eleanor's illness threatened to consume the little money he had

in hand. He saw, however, how impolitic it would
be for him to give way, and he resolved to bestir
himself as soon as his wife should be better. He
offered up a short but fervent prayer to Heaven for
assistance, and afterwards found himself both consoled and encouraged.

Eleanor lingered on in her illness, and as it continued their finances proportionately diminished. At
last the whole of their ready money was expended, and
Ambrose was obliged to sell their furniture and other
effects piece by piece to procure the bare means of
subsistence. One thing, however, perfectly consoled
him, Eleanor's health began to return rapidly, and
at last she was even able to take part in the house-
hold duties.

Ambrose now determined on paying a visit to his
old professor, Father Theodore, to consult him as
to what steps he should take. Father Theodore
received him with great kindness, and listened with
much patience, till Ambrose informed him that
Eleanor had been put to the torture. Father Theodore could at first hardly believe him, but when
Ambrose assured him it was a fact, the indignation
of the kind-hearted old man knew no bounds. He
even expressed himself in terms hardly suited to the
respect it was his duty as a monk to use when speaking of such a dignitary of the Church as the Bishop
of Winchester. When he had somewhat calmed
down, he took Ambrose to the Abbot and made him
repeat his story. The Abbot was as much surprised

as Father Theodore had been, and was possibly as indignant, but as he was a prudent man he did not express it.

Ambrose remained in the monastery for some time while the two monks were deliberating what might be done for him. At last the Abbot proposed that Ambrose should settle in the neighbourhood of the monastery, and they would throw in his way whatever practice they could.

"It is the best thing you can do, my son," said Father Theodore. "I am getting old and infirm, and should occasionally be glad to have some one on whom I could rely to take part of my duties. Your friend Father Peter is now such a martyr to the rheumatism that he will be able to offer you but little annoyance; and besides, I think we are strong enough here to neutralise any bad influence on his part. There are several families of respectable merchants, as you know, whose country houses are in the vicinity, and I have no doubt you will do very well."

Ambrose was so well pleased with the advice he had received that on leaving the monastery, and even before going home, he arranged with a respectable woman for a part of her house, and the next day he and his wife brought with them the few things which remained to them, and entered on possession of their new lodgings.

Things now took a turn with Ambrose greatly for the better. True, he did not at first get many affluent patients, but among the poor he was greatly liked.

The worthy Abbot watched him narrowly, and was day by day more pleased with his behaviour. He had not been settled in the neighbourhood of the monastery more than three months, when a wealthy old nobleman came to reside there. He was in very bad health, and was aware that his end was approaching. For that reason he wished to live near the Abbot, who was his spiritual adviser. This nobleman required daily the assistance of a surgeon, and the Abbot recommended Ambrose for that purpose, as Father Theodore never left the monastery in wet or cold weather. Ambrose was soon much liked by his new patient, who paid him liberally for his attendance. Nor did the benefit Ambrose derived from his patient stop there. The nobleman had a daughter whose husband was in daily attendance on the King. This lady used to come frequently with her children to see her father, and on more than one occasion she requested Ambrose's advice on divers childish maladies which, she imagined, threatened them. She was much pleased with his manner and skill, but no further benefit arose to Ambrose for some time from her acquaintance. At last the small-pox broke out with dreadful violence in the city, and singularly enough the disease which had indirectly brought on Ambrose so much misfortune, was the first step to his subsequent success. The two children of this lady were seized with the disease, and she begged the nobleman, her husband, to call Ambrose in to attend them. He complied with her request, and for the first time in his life Ambrose had the good fortune of attending on the family of a lady of quality. The two children suffered severely from the disease, but thanks to the skill of their leech they ultimately recovered. The lady was so much pleased with her doctor, that she introduced him to others of her acquaintance, and in a short time he became celebrated. He now removed from Bermondsey to the City, and took a handsome house, vastly different from the obscure lodgings he had hitherto occupied. At Father Theodore's death he stepped into the whole of his practice, and at last was called upon to attend the King in a serious malady, from which, however, under the care of Ambrose, he recovered.

Although Ambrose was now wealthy, he was by no means a niggard. He was not only kind to the poor as their doctor, but Eleanor, who acted as his almoner, was equally liberal in the dispensation of his charity. They lived beloved and respected by all who knew them, having but one sorrow—they had no family.

\*         \*         \*         \*         \*

We must now return to Ambrose, after the death of his dear wife. We have already narrated that on the afternoon of the second day he called upon Master Walter; and when he left the house it was to visit some sick poor, who were in urgent need of his assistance. It was nearly eight o'clock before he entered his own house, and he then found that his

servants had prepared some refreshment for him.
He sat down to the table and tried to eat, but it was
in vain, not a morsel could he swallow. He at last
gave up the attempt, and sought the chamber of his
dead wife. She was stretched on the bed in her
grave clothes, ready for her interment the next day.
Two corpse candles burnt by the head of her coffin,
and by her side was seated a nurse, whose duty it
was to watch the dead body. The poor woman was
pale and fatigued, and in a short time Ambrose
remarked her condition.

"You appear tired," said he. "I think you had
better go and lie down, and I will remain here."

She thanked him, but declined the offer.

"You are tired and ill yourself, sir," said she;
"you have not slept for several nights, and you will
make yourself ill if you do not take some rest.
Remember your illness would be as great a loss to
others as yourself."

Ambrose was forced to admit the truth of the
woman's reasoning, and he left the room for the
purpose of taking a little rest. He stretched himself on his bed but could not sleep. The immensity
of his sorrow was still before him, and he could not
close his eyes. He remained quiet, however, till it
was midnight, when he rose from his bed determined to pass the remainder of the night in prayer
beside his wife's corpse. He sought her chamber,
and insisted on the nurse going to her bed. The
woman, finding he would not be disobeyed, left him,

and Ambrose seated himself on the chair she had occupied. His thoughts were now fixed on her he had lost, and he gave them full rein, for there was nothing to distract his attention as the streets were now quiet, and all was silent as the grave she was shortly to repose in.

His thoughts now wandered over various episodes of their married life, from their first struggles to gain sufficient for their subsistence to the celebrity he had afterwards attained. He thought of her many virtues, her piety, and the warmth of her love for him alone, even exceeding the love of women. He looked for some moments on her dead form with a look of intense affection, and then rising from his seat he bent over the bed, and placing his lips on her cold brow, gave her a long and loving kiss.

"Eleanor, my dear wife," he said, "now that I have lost you I shall never know a happy moment.

You were to me as the breath of my life, and the whole sum of my earthly happiness; how can I ever live without you?"

He here gave vent to a burst of impassioned grief, and sinking on his knees he buried his face in his hands, which rested on the side of the bed. He

now wept bitterly, and without restraint. Suddenly
he fancied he felt the pressure of a hand on his
shoulder, but his sorrow was so overwhelming it
was only as a fancy. But the pressure continued,
and with added weight. Surprised, yet hardly be-
lieving in its reality, he slowly raised his head, and
saw standing behind him his wife in her grave-
clothes, her hand on his shoulder.

He imagined at first that it was her spirit, and
was on the point of praying to her as he would have
prayed to an angel, but the continued pressure on his
shoulder proved to him that it was her form in reality.
He now thought she must have been in a swoon, and
rose joyfully from his knees and clasped her in his
arms. But his joy vanished, for he clasped the unmistakeable substance of a corpse. He gazed at her
for a moment, utterly bewildered, but yet not terrified. He turned her gently towards the light and
looked in her face. There was no doubting the
reality, Death had there set his seal so fixedly that
the man of science could not be mistaken.

He now thought he must be dreaming some terrible dream, and he gazed round the room to assure
himself that he was awake. But again the reality
of the corpse he clasped in his arms proved to him
that it was no vision.

"Eleanor, my beloved wife, speak to me," he exclaimed, but not the slightest appearance of life
came over her pallid features. He now led her to a
seat, his arm round her waist, while she mechanically

yielded to his pressure and walked with him. Seated, she remained motionless; her eyes only had opened, but there was no life in them.

Ambrose placed his hand on his brow and re-flected what he should do. The idea again recurred to him that she was half-recovered from a swoon, and he resolved to bring a restorative from his laboratory to re-animate her entirely. But how to accomplish it? He feared if he left her she might fall, but on turning his eyes towards her he perceived that she sat quietly, as not requiring his assistance to support her. He removed the arm he had round her waist, and found that his surmise was correct, and that he could leave her.

Cautiously and in the dark, he found his way through an ante-room into a small laboratory. It was lighted from a window which looked into a court at the back of his house. The night, though tempestuous and very rainy, was, in consequence of the moon being near the full, sufficiently light to allow him to distinguish on a shelf the medicine he wanted. It was a restorative he was in the habit of using when life appeared to be sinking. He had succeeded in reaching it, and had turned again to seek the death-chamber, when, resolute man of science as he was, he started back in amazement. Close to his side, though without touching him, stood Eleanor, motionless and silent, and most singularly perceptible in the faint light of the moon. He gazed at her face for a moment and then recovered himself.

"Eleanor, my dearest wife," he said, gently placing one arm round her waist and with the hand of the other carrying the restorative, "Eleanor, my dearest, come back with me."

Slowly he threaded his way through the two rooms back into the death-chamber. She walked without difficulty, yielding to the pressure of his arm as he guided her. He reached the long seat on which they had been seated, and gently set her down beside him. He quickly seized a small cup, and poured in it some of the restorative, which he placed to her lips. But in vain: not a drop did she swallow; she sat there motionless as before.

He placed his finger on her pulse, and held it there for some minutes; his faculties were stretched to the utmost pitch of sensibility to distinguish the beating, but without  success. The dead arm remained motionless between his fingers. He took the highly polished little silver mirror his wife had used in her chamber, and held it to her lips, but not the slightest cloud appeared on it. He pressed his hand on her heart, but not a throb answered to it.

The physician now stood aghast, for his science plainly availed him nothing. Still, before admitting he was helpless, he leant his head forward on his

hand and thought over his position. Could he by
any means restore animation to his wife? There
was no pulse, there was no action of the heart, there
was not the slightest symptom of consciousness.
She was to all appearance, if the word imply not
a contradiction, an animated corpse. Her spirit, he
was assured, was with the blessed, and that afforded
him consolation; but what power could have given her
remains the faculty of movement it was impossible
for him to divine. Beyond the way in which she had
risen from her bed, approached him, and followed
him into the laboratory, she appeared deprived of
all movement except the power of sustaining herself
upright. She now sat by his side, perfectly capable
of holding herself in the position she was placed in,
yet in every other respect a corpse. There could be
no doubt on the subject,—she was under the influence of magic, and it was in the power of Heaven
alone to relieve her.

Near him against the wall was placed a picture
of the Virgin, before which night and morning his
dear Eleanor had been accustomed to kneel in prayer.
Before it he resolved to offer up a supplication
that the form of his wife might be released from the
enchantment that was on her. He cast a glance at
her, and saw that there was no danger in leaving
her: so he rose from his seat, and on the cushion
which she had so often knelt on before the picture, he
placed himself in the attitude of prayer. He prayed
that through the mediation of the Virgin the corpse

of his wife might be allowed to repose in peace, and
that at the termination of his mortal pilgrimage
he might be allowed to rest beside her. Should the
Virgin kindly listen to his supplication, he would
for the future consider himself dead to the world
and pass his life in seclusion, using all his efforts in
the service of God and for the welfare and comfort
of the poor.

He had hardly concluded his prayer when he felt
the soft pressure of a hand on his shoulder. He
raised his head and saw his dead wife standing by
his side. She bent over him, and pressing her lips
on his brow imprinted on it a kiss. The death-cold
contact on his brow seemed to thrill through him,
conveying a sensation of solemn awe, but without one
particle of terror. The effect was supernatural. The
kiss seemed the acceptance of his offer to leave the
world during his natural life and to be united to her
in the grave. He arose from his knees, and took
his wife round the waist to reconduct her to her seat,
but she moved not. He clasped her closer, or she
would have fallen. All power of sustaining herself
was lost, and she was again the natural corpse.
Ambrose, as soon as he was aware of the fact, bore
her carefully to the bed, laying her in the position
he had found her in when he had first entered the
room. He then placed himself on his knees beside
her, and prayed earnestly that her rest might no
more be disturbed. He felt as he prayed that his
petition had been heard, and gratefully he thanked

the Virgin for her mediation. But still he felt the impression of his wife's lips on his brow as clearly and unmistakeably as at the moment she stooped over him and kissed him. The feeling gave him no sorrow, but rather a strange sense of satisfaction, as it told him his offer to retire from the world had been accepted, and that after his death he should repose by the side of his beloved Eleanor. He continued praying until daylight, when the nurse entered the room. For some moments he remained in doubt whether he should leave the chamber, but he felt so positive that his wife's rest would not be again disturbed that at last he yielded to the woman's entreaties and left her.

Ambrose did not seek his chamber, but left the house for the purpose of postponing the funeral for

some days. In this he found no difficulty. No explanations were asked him, and he proffered none; not a word of the terrible night he had passed did he confide to any person.

At midnight he again sought his wife's chamber, and having dismissed the nurse, he kissed, as the night before, his wife on the forehead, but she re-

mained perfectly motionless, and he fervently thanked
the Virgin for it. For five nights did he keep watch
in the same manner without anything supernatural
occurring, and on the sixth day she was interred.
When her body was being lowered into the grave,
however, and he bent forward, broken-hearted, to
take one last look at the coffin which contained her,
he felt again the pressure of her lips on his brow as
clearly and palpably as on that terrible night he had
passed with her. The sensation had never quitted
him, but now the kiss was clearly and distinctly repeated. The feeling at the moment was one of satisfaction, not that it was necessary to remind him of
his promise, but that the relation between Eleanor
and himself remained, though she was now in her
grave.

From that moment he did not shed a tear. He
returned calmly to his own house, and deliberately
occupied himself with his affairs, determining in what
manner he would dispose of his effects, and in what
way he could relinquish his practice among the rich.
After having in part arranged his plan, he spent the
remainder of the day until evening in visiting and
prescribing for the poor, and that night he slept
calmly and soundly.

In the course of a few days Ambrose had made
over his practice to another physician, and had sold
almost everything he possessed. He then waited on
the King and informed him of his intention of entering the monastery in which he had been educated.

He prayed his Majesty to relieve him from his appointment of Court Physician, telling him at the same time that the doctor he had nominated as his successor was in every respect his equal in ability The King heard his physician with great sorrow, and with much condescension expressed his high respect for Ambrose, and the meeting terminated. Ambrose shortly afterwards entered the monastery, endowing it with all his wealth, which was very considerable. He lived for seven years after this, continuing punctual in all observances of his church, and occupying the remainder of his time in attending on the physical wants of the poor in the neighbourhood. When he died he carried with him to the grave the love and respect of all who knew him. His end was tranquil and painless, and his last wishes to be buried beside his dear wife were obeyed by the brethren of the monastery, all of whom, with a large number of the poor, attended his corpse to the grave.

# VIII.

## THE KING'S BALL.

WHILE these terrible scenes were being enacted in the house of the physician, a very different series of events was taking place in the family of the merchant. The doctor had hardly quitted the house after his visit to Master Walter when Bertha began to make preparations for the ball. In these she was assisted by the young lady already mentioned in connection with the tale of the "Ring of Frastrada" and two servant girls. The toilet of a young lady in those days took far less time than in these. Bertha, with only three assistants, was occupied but two hours at it before she left her room; and, more than that, to her great credit it should be stated, when her friends arrived she did not keep them waiting a moment.

It is no flattery to say that when Bertha entered the saloon to show herself to her father she appeared really beautiful—and she knew it. Her dress was of the latest mode and the most magnificent description, and it became her wonderfully well. The head-dress was of the newest and most becoming form, and had lately been imported from France by Monsieur Petitchose, who assured her it was the only one of the kind in England, so that she would be without a competitor. It not only suited the contour of her countenance admirably, but also allowed her superb back hair to be seen to the greatest advantage, slightly covering it, but yet allowing its glossy raven colour and abundant quantity to be heightened in beauty rather than concealed. Her front hair she wore simply turned off from the forehead, permitting her intellectual brow as well as her temples to be seen. The head-dress in front consisted only of two lappets of lace—but such lace!—which met in the centre of the head just above the forehead, and then fell down on each side over her shoulders. Her back hair was held in a network of gold thread strung with pearls of large size, their whiteness contrasting admirably with her dark hair, which again harmonised with her clear pale complexion. The head-dress alone must have cost the merchant a fortune. Her dress itself consisted of a bodice and skirt of the richest blue satin. Her father had lately received from Italy a vast consignment of valuable silks of different descriptions, and he had set aside this satin for his daughter's dress as being superior to all the others. In shape the bodice fitted her closely. It was cut square in front, and beneath it was seen a chemisette of the finest Mechlin lace. This in itself was a novelty, as the turnovers, bordered with fur, which reached from the back of the neck to the girdle in front were still worn by a majority of the ladies who had been invited to the ball. The bodice was splendidly embroidered with rich gold thread, and a band of gold lace went round the square in front. Her sleeves were long and open from half way between the shoulder and the elbow, showing beneath them an inner tight-fitting sleeve of white satin embroidered with silver thread. Her skirt was ample and long, yet not quite so long as to conceal entirely her small dancing shoes of rich velvet embroidered in gold.

When Bertha entered the room her father surveyed her with a look of intense pride, and for the moment evidently forgot the dreadful oppression he felt in his head. He had been reclining in a sort of easy-chair, with his head leaning on his hand, but he rose from it when he saw his daughter advance. His eye dilated with pleasure at the magnificent appear-  ance she made, and he said to her, " Bertha, my dear, you will have no rival to-night, or my fatherly love must strongly mislead me."

"I am afraid it does, father," said Bertha; but the expression of her countenance showed no fear of the kind.

It would be impossible to say how long her father's gaze of admiration would have lasted, for it was broken a few minutes after her entry into the room by the arrival of the Lord Mayor. He and the Lady Mayoress had descended from their litter, and had entered the house to see Bertha before she went to the ball. They expressed themselves delighted with the appearance she made, and complimented her very highly upon it. The Lady Mayoress was particularly delighted, and examined every article in detail with great minuteness, somewhat to the annoyance of Bertha. After a delay of a few minutes the Lord Mayor reminded them that it was time they should leave for the palace, as there would probably be a great crowd there, and they might have to wait some time before they could obtain admittance. Bertha told them she was quite ready, but that she had left something in her room; she would not, she said, detain them a moment.

This statement of Bertha's was not true: the sole reason she had for leaving the room was to catch one glimpse of herself in the magic mirror. Taking with her a lamp, which she placed on a small table near the glass, she receded a short distance from it, that she might obtain a better view of her whole person. She remained for some moments regarding herself with an expression of great admiration.

Presently she said to her image reflected in the mirror :—

"I wish you could go to the ball to-night in my place, and that I, invisible, could follow you and hear the compliments that you cannot fail to receive."

She had no sooner uttered the words than the image deliberately stepped from the mirror and, taking up the lamp, left the room. But great as Bertha's surprise was in seeing her own semblance walk before her, it was doubled by the fact that she found she was invisible and without sub- stance; that, in truth, it was her spirit that was following the figure, not her person.

She followed the figure till it entered the sitting- room, when she had some slight reason to be dis- contented with it. Not only did she see it cast a glance of supreme contempt at the costume of the Lady Mayoress, a kind, amiable, motherly woman, who went to the ball quite as much to have the pleasure of being near Bertha as for the ball itself, but she also remarked with great sorrow the look of impatience it gave at the warm commendations her father passed upon it.

The time had now arrived for them to leave; the Lord Mayor first conducted the false Bertha with great gallantry to her litter, and then returned for his wife. The party, being all in readiness, started for the palace, which they reached without accident or inconvenience of any kind: no easy feat, considering the crowded state of the streets.

As it would render our narrative somewhat confused if in the adventures at the ball we made a difference between the true and false Bertha, the reader is requested to bear in mind we shall describe the adventures of the false Bertha as those of our heroine, who followed her invisibly.

When they first entered the palace they were conducted by footmen into a magnificent room in which was spread what fashionable society in those days called the supper, but which in fact consisted of slight delicacies placed for the refreshment of the guests on their entrance, the principal repast of the evening being the rere-supper or banquet, which would not take place before midnight. In the room they found several of the guests already assembled, many of the ladies tasting, in great moderation, confectionery and sweets, which were handed to them by gallants, who profited by the opportunity to form acquaintanceship with young ladies, whom they invited to be their partners in the dance afterwards. A bevy of these gentlemen immediately surrounded

Bertha on her entrance, and pressed their services on her with great assiduity. She received their homage with much courtesy and condescension, but in reply to their requests to dance with them, she regretted that she could not at that moment decide, as she was already engaged for several dances, but she hoped in the course of the evening that she should find herself disengaged, and she would then accept their invitations with pleasure. The fact is, that when Bertha was introduced at Court a certain young nobleman had particularly attracted her attention, and he had been the subject of much thought on her part ever since; and as the false Bertha had inherited from the real all her sentiments, she looked anxiously round for the individual who had had so marvellous an effect on her before pledging herself to dance with any other. Although Bertha kept her thoughts a profound secret, she had contrived, with that ingenuity which young ladies often show when similarly situated, to ascertain the name of the swain, who was no other than the young Lord Hastings, one of the most fashionable and attractive noblemen in England.

On his side he had been greatly struck by Bertha's appearance and manner, and had determined to make himself as agreeable to her at the ball as possible; not that he had fallen in love with her, for he was one of the most fickle and dissipated young men of the day, but solely from the desire to include among his many conquests so handsome a young girl. He had therefore paid particular attention this night to his personal appearance.

He was not in the room when Bertha entered it, but he arrived shortly afterwards. She did not at first see him, for he stood for some time aloof from the bevy of beaux who surrounded her; but as they one by one left her, she at last caught sight of him.

If his appearance was attractive the first time she saw him, it was doubly so on this occasion, so magnificent was his toilet.

He had been a long time in France, and he aped as much as possible the costume and manners of the young dandies he had been accustomed to mix with in Paris. On the night of the ball he wore his hair puffed out at the sides, with a little feather fastened in some way on the crown of his head. He had no beard, but a little blonde moustache, which he had dyed black to set off his fair complexion to greater advantage. A large ruff of the finest Mechlin lace, stiffly starched and at least nine inches in depth, was round his throat. He wore a tight-fitting waistcoat or jerkin of purple velvet, with small slashings of pink satin all over it, and buttoned with gold buttons from the throat to the waist, which was very long. On his shoulders, fastened by a silver cord, he wore a short blue satin cloak, which reached only to his elbows. About the hips his dress was puffed out with six or eight large puffings of satin. He wore loose small-clothes of the same coloured velvet as his jerkin, and these were also covered with small satin slashings, and terminated just below the knee with two rows of puffings of the smallest size.

All eyes were upon him when he advanced to speak to Bertha, whose heart at the moment beat so violently that she could hardly answer him. He addressed her with great gallantry, telling her how much pleasure it gave him to meet her again. He hoped she would allow him to escort her to the ball-room and be his partner in the first dance. Bertha, in reply, assured him it would give her great pleasure. He immediately took her hand to lead her from the room, and they proceeded upstairs together and were ushered into the ball-room.

As his Majesty had not yet arrived, and it was contrary to etiquette to begin dancing till he should be present, Lord Hastings profited by the opportunity to make himself more intimate with his partner.

"I do not know," he said, "from what reason, but I was afraid you would not be present to-night, and I feared I should not see you again."

"When did you ever see me?" said Bertha,

a

simulating surprise in the most natural manner possible.

"The day you were presented at Court; and I have never ceased to see you since."

Of course Bertha did not hear his Lordship's answer.

"Ah! Hastings," said a magnificently dressed young noble, who at the moment entered the room, "I perceive, as usual, you intend to be the star of the evening. No one it seems to me, can approach you."

"It has not been for lack of courage to attempt it, I see," said Hastings, casting a glance at the new comer's dress.

"Yes, courage, I admit; but pity it has not met with better success. Is your fair partner engaged for the second dance? If not, I shall be happy to offer myself."

"I trust she is," said Hastings, "and for the third and fourth as well, my dear Salisbury."

"Meaning," said Lord Salisbury, "that she is engaged to yourself. But it is rather cruel to others," he continued, addressing Bertha, " to allow Hastings to dance with you so often when so many ardently wish to have you as their partner."

Although Bertha, as we have frankly acknowledged, had a great admiration for Lord Hastings, at the same time she had no intention to allow her predilection to detract in any way from her womanly dignity; and she did not choose that Lord Hastings should think he could take such a liberty with her as to hinder her accepting another partner if she thought fit.

"I am only engaged for the first dance," said Bertha to Lord Salisbury, "and shall be happy to dance the second with you if you wish it."

Lord Salisbury warmly thanked her for conferring upon him such happiness, as he called it, while Lord Hastings stood by and spitefully bit his lip.

"Whom did I understand you to say that nobleman was," said Bertha, when Lord Salisbury had left them. "I noticed him at the Court, but I did not catch his name?"

"He is Lord Salisbury, an intimate friend of mine, and I really have a great friendship for the poor fellow, but unfortunately he is lamentably destitute of good breeding."

"In what way?" asked Bertha.

"For example, the manner in which he addressed us. Nothing could be more ill-bred than to intrude himself upon us when he saw we were engaged in conversation."

Poor Bertha made no answer. She saw no rudeness whatever in Lord Salisbury's behaviour, but she was afraid to say so lest she should betray her own ignorance of the manners of fashionable society. For some moments Lord Hastings continued silent, and then he broke out with—

"You cannot imagine how much you have hurt my feelings."

" How so ? " inquired Bertha.

" In remembering to have seen Salisbury at Court, and altogether forgetting me."

Bertha at the moment really pitied the poor fellow, and was racking her brain to say something consolatory in reply, when a flourish of trumpets as well as a simultaneous silence among the company warned them that the King was entering the ball-room. All, of course, made room for his Majesty, who graciously made the tour of the room, bowing or speaking condescendingly to all he knew.

When he approached Bertha he immediately recognised her, and asked after her father's health.

Bertha, with much hesitation in her manner, replied that her father was slightly better, but not yet sufficiently recovered to offer his services to his Majesty. She was overwhelmed at the notice the King had taken of her, as well as being aware that the eyes of the whole room were upon her,

" I am sorry for that," said the King, "for we miss him greatly from our Council Chamber," and he then passed on to a group of foreigners who had been invited to the ball.

" I did not know your father was one of the King's councillors," said Lord Hastings to Bertha.

" Oh yes," said Bertha, "but he has only lately been nominated, although his Majesty has been pleased to honour him already with especial notice ; " and then, wishing to make herself appear as aristocratic as possible in the eyes of his Lordship, she

continued, "and there is every probability of his
being Lord Mayor."

She gave a slight glance at Lord Hastings' face
to see how he received the news of this probable
accession of dignity to her family, and was both surprised and annoyed to find something like an expression of ridicule on it; but as at that moment
two citizens' wives passed them dressed in a most
absurd manner, she naturally supposed it was caused
by the appearance they made.

The King having made the round of the room, the
music sounded for a dance, and the gentlemen
taking their partners by the hand led them to their
places.   Lord Hastings was an excellent and graceful
dancer, and he flattered himself he should be able to
excite Bertha's admiration by his skill, but he was
doomed to be terribly disappointed.   His Majesty,
to please the citizens, chose for the first dance the
old-fashioned "Corale," a dance much in vogue with
the middle classes, but which had been banished
from the Court and from fashionable society generally.   In the "Corale" all stood up in a ring
dancing together, and occasionally changing partners, so that Lord Hastings had no opportunity to
make the effect he wished.   He contented himself,
however, with ridiculing the dancing of the others,
especially the ladies, to Bertha.   This he did with
great facility, as he had discovered that Bertha
spoke French fluently, and they conversed in that
language.

When the dance was over Lord Hastings led
Bertha to a seat, and there they continued their cri-
ticisms in French on the dress and manners of the
assembled company.　In fact, there was ample room
for their satire, for never was a more motley assem-
bly collected together.　Modes of a century old were
there mingled with those of the latest date imported from France.　Some of the citizens' wives
wore preposterously high caps, something like those
of the Normandy peasants, but grossly exaggerated;
such as had been banished from the Court at least
half a century before.　The dresses of many had
certainly belonged to their grandmothers, and had
possibly been worn at their weddings.　Among the
men there were the same discrepancies.　Some, such
as Lord Hastings and Lord Salisbury, were dressed
with exquisite taste after the fashion of the day,
while many of the senior aldermen had evidently
ransacked the long-laid-aside wardrobes of their
youth, and now appeared in all the splendour of
*L'habit du premier communion,* as Lord Hastings
cruelly termed it.

The next dance was called, and Lord Salisbury advanced to take his partner to her place.　As she left
Lord Hastings he cast an imploring glance in her
face which went direct to her heart.　She now felt
really angry with herself for having accepted Lord
Salisbury as a partner.　The dance had been changed
from the "Corale" to one of more modern date lately
imported from France, where each cavalier danced

with his partner and no other, resting occasionally,
as each couple felt tired, as in the present waltz.
It was during these rests that cavaliers then, as
now, attempted to make themselves agreeable to
their partners in conversation. Lord Salisbury was
by no means remiss on this point, keeping up a very
lively conversation with Bertha, and occasionally
putting in a remark which was intended to convey .
something more than simple gallantry, and thus
giving her to understand how much his feelings were
interested in her good opinion. Bertha, highly flattered, listened to him with pleased attention; but,
from time to time, she could not help casting a
glance at Lord Hastings, who, seated at the side of
the room, gazed at her steadily, with a mournfully
tender expression of countenance.

When the dance was over, Lord Salisbury walked
round the room with his partner for a short time,
making himself the while as agreeable as possible by
his conversation; but, in Bertha's opinion, he was
far behind his rival in intellectual powers. Again, his
ignorance of the French language lowered him considerably in her estimation, as lacking one of the
accomplishments for which Lord Hastings was so
remarkable, and thereby preventing her from making
certain little satirical or deprecatory remarks she was
occasionally inclined to pass on her neighbours without being understood by the bystanders.

Presently Lord Salisbury saw Lord Hastings approaching them, and, feeling his inferiority, with a

petty malice which did him but little credit, he conducted his partner to the Lady Mayoress, and placed her under her protection.   He knew perfectly well the aversion which Lord Hastings had for that lady, as well as for the citizens and their families generally.

But Lord Hastings, nothing daunted, approached Bertha as soon as his rival had left her, and craved her hand for the next dance, which she unhesitatingly promised him.   The dance soon after commenced, and Lord Hastings made the most of his time, saying all the sweet nothings he could think of with such persuasive eloquence that poor Bertha was not proof against them, but began to feel the warmest interest in her admirer.   She did not, as in the last dance, cast frequent glances at her late partner, who sat moodily apart from his brilliant rival.   She did not once look towards him. Had she never seen him he could not have been more indifferent to her than he was at that moment.

As the evening passed away Lord Salisbury had again an opportunity of dancing with Bertha.   Instead of making himself agreeable, he then had the bad taste to vent his spite against his rival, saying all the ill-natured things of him he could think of. This was little to Bertha's taste, though somewhat flattering to her vanity.   She could easily perceive that the cause of his ill-humour was simply jealousy.

Suddenly the thought struck her that if she encouraged him a little, it might have the effect of making

Lord Hastings express himself in more explicit terms
than he had hitherto done. He had paid her the
warmest compliments and had hinted at the susceptible state of his heart, but he had hardly spoken
so clearly on the subject as he might have done.

Bertha now appeared perfectly delighted with the
wit and humour of the remarks which fell from the
lips of her partner, whom she encouraged by every
means in her power to continue his conversation.
With great tact she gave him subjects to discourse on
when he seemed to flag (for it must be allowed the
genius of his Lordship was by no means of the first
order), and when the dance was finished she took his
arm and walked with him round the room, talking
most agreeably the while.

At last she complained of fatigue and requested
him to conduct her to the Lady Mayoress. She
seated herself immediately by the lady's side, taking
good care to leave sufficient room for Lord Salisbury
to sit down at the other side should he be so disposed. His Lordship had sufficient wit to profit by
the opportunity, and the pair sat talking together
with great animation on subjects connected with
the ball and the company. Presently Lord Hastings
advanced and asked her hand for the next dance, but
Bertha excused herself, saying she felt fatigued and
should not dance again until after the banquet.
Her disappointed suitor retired with deep sorrow
marked on his handsome countenance. He seated
himself some distance off, and cast most expressive

glances at her, all of which she pretended not to notice, though in reality not one of them was lost upon her.

At last Lord Hastings rose, and approaching Bertha, said to her, in his most tender and winning tones :—

" If you are not engaged with a cavalier to hand you into supper, you would greatly oblige me if you would allow me the honour."

" Certainly, and with great pleasure," said Bertha, graciously; and Lord Hastings retired with an expression of supreme happiness on his countenance, while his rival's pleasure fell in exactly the same proportion.

Now this was exactly what Bertha wished. Little as she had hitherto mixed with the world, she instinctively knew how much might be said at that meal. All her plans had fallen out precisely as she desired, and her object now was to put Lord Salisbury in good humour again.

" I thought," said he, " I should have had the pleasure of conducting you into supper."

" I had not the remotest idea you wished it," said Bertha, " or I would certainly have declined Lord Hastings' invitation."

" Indeed I do wish it," said he, " and ardently, too. Could you not put him off? I will take the risk upon myself."

" That would hardly be courteous on my part," said Bertha. " I much regret you did not express your wish sooner; but it is too late now."

"Are you engaged for the first dance after supper?" he inquired; "if not, pray dance it with me."

"Most willingly," said Bertha; "I will hold myself engaged for it."

This put Lord Salisbury in good humour again, and everything passed off agreeably till supper was announced, when Lord Hastings advanced, and offering Bertha his hand, led her into the banqueting-room.

The rere-supper or banquet was one of the most magnificent affairs of the kind ever given in England. It was spread out in a spacious hall so brilliantly illuminated that it dazzled the eyes of the company when they entered it. In the centre of the room were two long lateral tables, and a third at the farther extremity was placed transversely near the wall opposite the entrance doors. His Majesty knowing the liking of his faithful citizens for good living, had directed the Lord Chamberlain that nothing should be wanting to give *éclat* to the feast, and that nobleman, to the best of his abilities and those of his subordinates, had carried out his Majesty's orders even to the minutest details. The guests, without exception, were furnished with a knife "clean scoured," and every lady with a horn spoon.

The rere-supper of course embraced every delicacy of the season. On the longitudinal tables were placed the lighter viands and confectionery, such as

would be likely to tempt the ladies. There were
fruit tarts of every description, chickens farced
and roasted, sparrows in almond milk, and jellies
served on silver platters. There were also many
dishes of great delicacy, unfortunately no longer
found on our tables, such as the *pommes d'orange*;
which, by-the-way, did not consist of oranges
in any shape, but of pounded pig's liver, delicately
made up with cinnamon, apples, and currants,
bound together in a ball with the whites of eggs,
and then covered with parsley and coloured with
indigo and saffron, and glazed over. These were
very delicate eating and much patronised by well-bred
middle-aged ladies; while their daughters partook
of the still more delicate Mawnenè, made of almonds
blanched and powdered and then mixed with white
wine, to which were added the brawn of pheasants
very finely pounded, and ground rice. The whole
was afterwards boiled, and powder of ginger, cloves,
cinnamon, and sugar mixed with it; and then, says
the recipe, "take rice and parboil it, and add it to
the rest; colour the whole with sandal wood, and
pour it out on dishes to cool. Then take the grains
of pomegranates and stick in it, or almonds or
pines fried in grease, and lastly strew sugar over
all."

There were also on these tables cream of almonds
and delicate roast squirrel garnished with roasted
larks. Payne puffe, wood doves, tortons in paste,
quails, and goldfinches, and in fact everything that

could tempt the more fastidious appetites of the
ladies.

On the transverse tables, especially intended for
gentlemen without partners, but at which also were
placed some middle-aged ladies, accidentally of
course, were ranged the *pièces de résistance*. There
was a magnificent wild boar roasted whole, legs of
pork, baked swans, mallards, capons roasted in
syrup, roasted pigs, herons, tarts of flesh, hedgehogs
stewed in wine (these last were particularly patronised by elderly gentlemen with *blasé* appetites),
roasted peacocks glazed with the whites of eggs and
cooked in their skins.

Every kind of fish the British seas produced was
also there, from the magnificent baked porpoise to
the delicate sprat.

Nor were the more artistic productions of the cook
wanting on the transverse tables. There was the
celebrated boar brasée, for which the English cooks
of the period were so renowned. It was made of the
ribs of a boar half boiled and then roasted, and when
cooked chopped up small and placed in a saucepan
with fresh beef broth, to which white wine, cloves,
mace, pines, currants, and powdered pepper were
added. After slowly boiling for some time, it was
poured into a pan and mixed with chopped onions
well fried in grease. The whole was then coloured
with sandal wood and saffron, and as it cooled a
small quantity of powdered cinnamon and a little
vinegar were added.

In fact all the viands offered to the guests at the banquet were of the most *recherché* description, and, could the comparison have been made, would have put to shame the meaner kitchens of the Reform and Carlton Clubs.

Nor were wines wanting of quality capable of competing with the viands. They were all of a most costly description, and from every country. There were red and white wines, claret, Malmsey, Osey, and Rhenish wines, also London beer and Kentish ale, which were served to the guests when called for by a host of footmen arrayed in magnificent liveries.

That nothing might be wanting to lend enchantment to the scene, a band of trumpeters, at least twenty in number, played most vigorously on their instruments during the repast. They had straight trumpets of a form somewhat similar to those used by the guards of our old mail-coaches, but longer and far more sonorous.

Bertha and Lord Hastings were seated at the farther extremity of one of the longitudinal tables in such a position as enabled them to see a great portion of the room. He was exceedingly gallant, choosing for her the most delicate dishes; in fact, paying her every attention in his power. He ate with an excellent appetite himself, and was by no means sparing of the wines offered to him; indeed, as Bertha noticed, he drank somewhat freely. After a short time the pair found their tongues, and they conversed together with great animation in the French language. The discourse of Lord Hastings was of a mixed character. Sometimes he warmly complimented his partner, and informed her how much he was struck with her charms; sometimes he made satirical remarks on the company present.

"Do you see that fellow opposite," he said, "tearing his food to pieces with his fingers? You must really pardon me if I say the citizens have yet much to learn in good breeding," while at the same time he held some boar's head on his own platter delicately with the fingers of his left hand, and made use of his knife with the right. "Look at that Alderman," he continued, "attacking the baked porpoise; why one would think he had never seen a dish of the  kind in his life before, and was afraid he should never see another. By-the-by, I half suspect that fellow must in his heart be a cannibal, or he never could swallow a mouthful of an animal that bore so strong a resemblance to himself."

"But," said Bertha, "you must not imagine that all citizens are so savage as he is. I am sure if my poor father were here he would be able to conduct himself with as much propriety as any nobleman in the land."

"Of that I am perfectly persuaded," said his Lordship; "but then we ought not to rank a merchant of his standing with such boors as we see around us. Look at that fellow opposite, in the old-fashioned velvet coat——"

"It is paid for, at any rate," said the individual alluded to, in excellent French; "can your Lordship say as much for your own?"

Lord Hastings thought it better not to hear this remark. He turned his head aside to order one of the footmen to bring Bertha a dish from the other end of the table, pointing it out to the man with great care, but the blush and annoyance which at the same time appeared on his countenance proved that his opposite neighbour's observation had struck home. The anxiety he at the moment showed in Bertha's behalf was simply to conceal the vexation he really felt.

Bertha, however, heard the remark perfectly well, and, strange as it may appear, without the least sorrow, for it seemed to place the relative positions of his Lordship and herself more on a level. To do her justice, she did not reason on the subject, but she arrived spontaneously at the conclusion that there was less social difference in their respective grades. That he was poor she had never heard, although she knew he was not considered wealthy; while on her side she was heiress to wealth greater, or as

great, as that possessed by any lady among the
nobility.

When the dish was brought, Lord Hastings again
seated himself by Bertha's side, and they conversed
together, now in English, on different commonplace
subjects, the remark of their opposite neighbour
having made his Lordship far more circumspect in
his speech. It was evident, however, his annoyance
continued, and to drown it he took more wine. His
conversation was now forced and unnatural, but
soon changed again into a gayer tone, for the gentleman who had made the exceedingly rude observation had risen from the table and seated himself
in another part of the room.

As soon as he had gone, Lord Hastings again
began to converse in French, but in a somewhat
more subdued tone. He began by simply asking
her whether her father would be offended by his
calling at the house. Bertha, in reply, assured
him that she was certain her father would consider
himself flattered by the visit of a nobleman of his
Lordship's position. He then changed the subject to
family matters, asking her what had detained her
brother from coming to the ball; he regretted it,
he said, as he should have had much pleasure in
making his acquaintance. Bertha replied that she
had neither brother nor sister; the only relative she
had in the world, with the exception of her uncle,
being her father.

This was just the point Lord Hastings wished to

arrive at, and he had made the remark about her brother, of whom of course he had heard nothing, simply to find out the state of her family connections.

"Does your uncle reside in London?" he inquired.

"Yes, he is on the livery of the Fishmongers' Company, and expects soon to be made Master. He is rather an eccentric old bachelor, and we see him but seldom."

His lordship made a slight grimace at the mention of the eccentric fishmonger, which Bertha noticed. It annoyed her extremely, and she blamed herself sincerely for her clumsiness in naming her uncle. There had really been no occasion for it, as he was, after all, only her mother's half-brother.

Lord Hastings now called for another glass of wine, evidently to drown the fishmonger in. After he had drank it he again commenced his conversation with Bertha in a warmer strain even than before; and it is more than probable it might have ended in a formal declaration, had not a simultaneous rising of the company from the tables stopped him. He, however, offered his hand to Bertha, to conduct her into the ball-room, profiting by the occasion to press hers in a perfectly perceptible manner, to which Bertha made no objection.

They had only been in the ball-room a few minutes when the music sounded the prelude to a dance, and Lord Hastings immediately led his partner, who appeared to have utterly forgotten her previous engagement, to her place. Lord Salisbury, however, was by no means so oblivious, and advancing to claim Bertha's hand, reminded her of her previous promise to him. Bertha readily admitted she was in error, and was on the point of quitting Lord Hastings, though with evident regret, when her partner showed that he had no intention of resigning her so easily.

"Salisbury," he said, "I was this lady's courtier at supper, and, as you must be aware, I am entitled to dance the first dance with her afterwards."

"Nonsense," said Lord Salisbury, "I was engaged to her before supper, and unless she objects to keep her promise, I shall certainly not resign my right to her hand."

Bertha now perceived that the eyes of the by-standers were on her, and, being unwilling to cause any disagreement or interruption, she said that she was most sorry to have made such a mistake, but in consequence of it she should decline dancing that dance with anyone; and she at once left the two noblemen, and sought the protection of the Lady Mayoress, who was seated in a distant part of the room.

Although Bertha had intended to stop all further dispute between her partners by refusing to dance, it had by no means the effect she anticipated; on the contrary, each was enraged the more against the other.

"Hastings," said Lord Salisbury, "your behaviour more resembles that of a clown than a nobleman.

You knew perfectly well I was engaged to the girl, and you had no right to interfere."

"Salisbury," said Lord Hastings, "that is not

exactly the style of language in which I am accustomed to be addressed, and I must request you will withdraw the expression. I shall, however, not say more tonight. I trust to-morrow you will be in a better tone of mind, and make the apology due to me."

"Do not trouble yourself to wait till to-morrow," said Lord Salisbury. "The remark I made was in the anger of the moment. I am now calmer, and in cool blood I beg to repeat it. Your conduct, I say, is more that of a clown than a nobleman."

Lord Hastings could not restrain himself at this insult, and was on the point of expressing himself in a very indignant tone, when a bystander touched him on the arm, and reminded him that his Majesty was still in the room, and that any altercation would be most indecorous in his presence. Both the young men felt the propriety of the remark, and Lord Hastings proposed to his adversary that they should leave the ball-room for some other locality where they could

talk over the matter without fear of interruption.
Lord Salisbury immediately assented, and the pair
left the room and sought a small side chamber,
which had been used before supper for the purpose
of gaming. The room was now empty, but the dice
boxes were still on the table.

Bertha, though seated by the Lady Mayoress, kept
her eye fixed with intense anxiety on the disputants.
When they left the room, which she could perceive
they did in no very amiable state of mind, her curiosity became still greater. She controlled herself
for some time, however, till at length her anxiety to
know what was taking place became greater than she
could endure. Accordingly, on some pretext invented
at the moment, she left the Lady Mayoress's side, and
made her way round the room, avoiding the dancers
as she best could, until she reached the door by
which her admirers had left it. She strolled by
chance down a corridor, and at last distinguished in
a room the voice of Lord Hastings.

" Do you not think it a pity, Salisbury," he said,
"that after the number of years we have been
friends we should end our friendship by cutting each
other's throats, and about such a girl as that?
Neither of us in reality, I am sure, cares one straw
about her."

" That's all very well, Hastings ; but for all that
she was to be my partner, and you had no right to
interfere. I care no more about her than you do,
but I do not choose to give her up."

"I do not .suppose you do care about her," said Lord Hastings, "save only for the sake of amusing yourself; but you see after what has taken place I cannot resign her either, that is to say, not upon a threat. To avoid all dispute between us, I will propose that we throw for her with the dice. If you throw highest I will withdraw; and if I throw highest you shall leave the field open to me. What do you say to my proposition?"

"I accept it with all my heart," said Lord Salisbury. "Shall I throw first?"

"By all means, and may good luck attend you; for, to tell the truth, I am getting tired of being made love to in the manner I have been this evening, as well as of hearing her talk about the probability of her father's being Lord Mayor, and her uncle the eminent fishmonger."

The sound of the dice rattling in the box now reached Bertha's ear.

"Ten," said Lord Salisbury.

Again the rattle was heard.

"Seven, by Jupiter!" said Lord Hastings. "Salisbury, the wench is yours. Now I hope we are friends again."

"Perfectly so," said Lord Salisbury.

Bertha made her way back to the ball-room in a state of mind little to be envied. She had hardly entered it, and had not yet reached the Lady Mayoress, when Lord Salisbury overtook her.

"Hastings," he said, "has resigned in my favour, and now you must dance with me."

Bertha could not answer him, but she greatly surprised him by the expression of intense indignation in her glance.

"What is the matter?" said he. "Have I offended you in any manner?"

Bertha, seeing the necessity of speaking, merely said, "I shall dance no more to-night."

"Pardon me," said Lord Salisbury, "but that will not be courteous. You know you are engaged to me."

Bertha made no excuse, and tried to pass on to her seat, but Lord Salisbury attempted to detain her.

"My lord," she said aloud, "you are neither acting like a nobleman nor a gentleman; I insist on your leaving me."

"If you are waiting for Hastings," he said, with something of a sneer, "you will be disappointed, for as I told you before he has given you up."

"Will nobody release me from this man?" said Bertha, looking around her.

Two or three gentlemen directly advanced, but their interference only put his Lordship more out of temper.

"I warn you," he said to the bystanders, "not to interfere with me; I am not a man to be insulted with impunity."

"I will seek redress of his Majesty himself," said Bertha, as she pushed through the crowd with an expression of countenance which showed that she had the courage to put her threat into execution.

"Salisbury, are you mad?" said a nobleman to him. "For Heaven's sake leave her alone or you will get yourself into trouble; remember what a favourite her father is with the King."

Lord Salisbury, angry as he was, had sense enough left to see the justice of the remark, and he immediately addressed Bertha:

"If I have offended you in any way, pray allow me to apologize. I assure you I had no intention of the kind."

"Then leave me," said Bertha, "and let me be troubled with no more impertinence either from you or your friend, or I promise you I will instantly appeal to his Majesty."

Lord Salisbury directly left her, and she resumed her seat beside the Lady Mayoress.

Although no longer annoyed either by Lord Hastings or his companion, Bertha did not resume her equanimity, notwithstanding that she attempted by her countenance to show she was in perfect good humour.

At last her patience could support her no longer, and she requested a friend of the Lord Mayor's to whom she was known to conduct her to her litter. With some difficulty it was found, and the gentleman having placed her in it, escorted her to her father's and left her.

When Bertha entered the house, there was some difficulty in awaking her waiting maid, who, being thoroughly tired, had fallen fast asleep. The girl at last arrived, and was somewhat alarmed at the expression of her mistress's countenance, but of course made no remark. She preceded Bertha upstairs, lighting her with a somewhat heavy lamp which she carried in her hand. When they had arrived at the mirror chamber, Bertha found she had dropped her cloak on the stairs, and desired the girl to go back and bring it, somewhat unreasonably taking the lamp from her hand, that she might not be left in the dark. The girl proceeded on her errand, and Bertha advanced mechanically towards the mirror. She gazed at her reflection for a moment, and the remembrance of the pleasure she had experienced at her brilliant appearance before she left for the ball came vividly before her. This again brought to her mind the different scenes of the evening, the pleasure she had felt before the supper, the agreeable dances she had had, the ambitious hopes she had nourished, and lastly, the terrible insult and disappointment she had experienced. On the last subject her mind dwelt especially, and as she thought over

it her passion rose in proportion, till at last, no
longer mistress of her actions, and in a fit of ungovernable fury, she raised the lamp she had in her
hand, and with all the force in her power, dashed
it against the mirror, which in a moment was shat-
tered into a hundred pieces, while the lamp, extinguished by the shock, fell to the ground, leaving the
chamber in total darkness. But the breaking of
the mirror had another effect; the real Bertha
who had invisibly followed the false one through
the whole of the evening, immediately returned
to her proper form and her image vanished.

It would be difficult to imagine two frames of mind
more directly different than that of the false Bertha
when she threw the lamp at the mirror, and that of
the real Bertha when she had resumed her form.
The one was impelled by the most unreasoning rage,
the other was mild, sorrowful, and subdued. She
waited with tears in her eyes till she heard the foot-
steps of the waiting-maid approaching her, and then
she said, "Joan, I have no light, try and find me
another." The girl at once obeyed her, finding
her way below as she best could in the dark,
and wondering in what manner the light had been
extinguished, but still more surprised at the altered
tone of her mistress.

Joan contrived with some little difficulty to find
another light, and returned with it to her mistress.
The girl uttered a cry of surprise when she saw
the mirror broken to pieces, the fragments strewed

upon the ground, but Bertha said not a word. She stood there silent and abashed before her hand-maid, and though wishing to give the girl some explanation of the accident was unable from pure shame to utter a word. She took the light from Joan's hand, and beckoned her to follow her into her chamber. As soon as Bertha had prepared herself for the night, she told the girl to leave her; and when the door was closed and bolted, she mentally recapitulated the events of the evening. She traced its history after her arrival at the palace, and every subject that occurred to her brought with it some painful reminiscence. She remembered the look of scorn which her semblance cast around her in the ante-chamber, before she went upstairs into the ball-room, at the dress and appearance of the citizens' wives and daughters there assembled, whose costumes were so far inferior to her own. She heard one lady say to another,—

"Did you see that Bertha de Courcey giving herself such airs and looking in such a contemptuous manner at my daughters? I remember the time when her father used to sweep out my father's shop. They have got on finely in the world certainly, but greater pride than theirs has had a fall."

"She must be a heartless creature," said another, "to come here dressed in that manner when her father is, as I understand on very good authority, on his death-bed at home."

"They were always a selfish set," said a third; "like father, like daughter. I have been told that when his father was dying, the son cared as little about him as his daughter does about hers."

The conversation was then taken up in a different part of the room by some citizens.

"How that girl is dressed out to-night," said one; "why, it must have cost a fortune to have purchased those things she has on."

"They can afford it," said a second; "I have no doubt it has been done out of the profits of the yew timber. Did you hear of that affair?"

"Did I hear of it?" said the other; "is there a man on 'Change who did not? A more rascally swindle, I believe, never was perpetrated. Is it true, by-the-bye, that the Bowyers Company intend commencing an action to set aside the whole affair?"

"I did not hear that," was the answer, "but I trust they will do so, for it was little better than a robbery, after all."

"I suppose," said one young man to another, "Bertha de Courcey will dance with none of us to-night. Since her father has been made one of the King's councillors she will not look at a gallant from the city."

"Dance with us, indeed!" was the reply; "I should say not. Do you see the eyes she is making at that French-looking doll, Lord Hastings? A fellow who is as poor as Job, without one of his virtues."

"She will have a precious catch if she gets him. I would sooner see my sister married to the poorest tradesman in London than to such a fellow as that. You might make a respectable and honest man out of the former, but nothing short of a miracle could work a reformation of the kind in Lord Hastings."

"Let us hope he will marry her, then," said the other, laughing; "it will be a just punishment to her for her contempt of those in her own station in life."

In the ball-room, poor Bertha met with no greater satisfaction than below; wherever she went it was her unhappy fate to hear depreciatory remarks on her imperious behaviour. It was noticed that not a citizen would she dance with the whole evening, and every gallant whom she refused added another to her detractors. But angry as were the young citizens, and annoying as were their remarks, they were harmless to those she heard uttered by the young ladies, many of whom it is more than probable had marked out for themselves a course of behaviour extremely similar to that pursued by the false Bertha.

In the supper-room even worse fortunes awaited her. Every gesture was remarked, and every one was severely criticised. But perhaps the most cruel of all were those observations elicited by the citizen whose dress had been noticed in so uncomplimentary a manner by Lord Hastings. This individual had amused himself by listening to the conversation which had been carried on by his Lordship. and Bertha in French, which language at last he had showed in so disagreeable a manner that he perfectly understood. When he left his seat, which he did some time before the supper was finished, he placed himself some distance off, but where he could still command a good view of the couple who had caused him so much chagrin by their remarks on his cloak. There he occupied himself by detailing to some young ladies the conversation he had overheard, and exaggerating it according to his fancy. He was listened to with great attention and interest, and their replies and remarks in return were even worse than those he had uttered.

The scene in the ball-room had also given Bertha much pain by the observations which it caused, and it was with a feeling of great satisfaction she followed the false Bertha to her litter.

When poor Bertha had gone through the events of the evening, she reflected what course she should pursue for the future, and what excuse or explanation she should make to her father about the broken mirror. On the first subject she soon came to a conclusion. It was simply to be less ambitious and more amiable for the time to come. She had a sufficiently just idea of her own good qualities to be certain that in adopting a different line of conduct she should be able to neutralise the bad impression which prevailed respecting her, and she resolved to be kind, amiable, and conciliatory to all.

With respect to the mirror, it was a far more diffi-

cult affair—she knew not what excuse to make. She
did not like to tell her father of the wonderful pheno-
menon which had occurred in her image leaving the
glass and going to the ball, lest she should not be believed; and still less did she like to acknowledge that
she herself had been in such an ungovernable fury
as to break it. At last she resolved to put off the
avowal till a later time. The next day they were to
leave for the country, and there she determined to
deliberate on the matter and follow the course she
should then consider the best suited for the occasion. She now remained more at peace with herself
till daylight, and when she rose she offered a prayer
to Heaven for assistance in carrying out the good
resolutions she had formed.

# IX.

## THE MIRROR BROKEN.

In consequence of the fatigue she had experienced at the King's ball, and the sleepless hours she had afterwards passed, Bertha de Courcey when she left her room seemed pale and exhausted. Her beauty, however, was by no means diminished; on the contrary, it was rather improved than otherwise. One blemish in her usual expression of countenance arose from the haughtiness of her natural disposition, but that had now vanished, and in its stead there was a subdued look of docility and amiability. The change which had come over her spirit was also apparent in the tone of her voice, which was now gentle and kindly. She occupied herself before breakfast in giving orders to the servants respecting the journey she and her father were about to take. She told them it was Master Walter's intention to start immediately after breakfast, and she requested them to have the mules and pack-horses with the luggage in readiness. This they promised should be strictly obeyed, wonder-

ing the while at the change which had come over
their young mistress's tone and manner. Having
given all her directions necessary for the journey,
Bertha went into the breakfast-room, and there
waited quietly till she should receive some message
from her father requiring her attendance in his
room.

But none came; and at last Bertha began to feel
somewhat uneasy at the delay, when suddenly the
door opened and Master Walter de Courcy entered
the room. Bertha when she saw him uttered a cry
of surprise, and not without cause. When she had
left her father the evening before, and he had risen
from his seat to bid her farewell, he did so with
great difficulty. He rested his head on his hand,
and it was some moments before he could speak, so
infirm was he. He now walked into the room with
a light step and head as erect as a man in the enjoy-
ment of perfect health. He advanced, laughing, towards his daughter, and, after kissing her affectionately, said to her: —

"What! did I startle you, my little Bertha? You
did not expect to see me down to breakfast, did
you?"

"In truth, father, I did not; but you make me
happy to see you look so much better;" and her
eyes filled with tears, for the remarks she had heard
the evening before at the ball respecting the health of
her father came at that moment to her mind.

"I certainly feel wonderfully better," said he;

t

" but, come, what have you for breakfast, for I am desperately hungry?"

Bertha again was surprised, as her father had not had the slightest appetite for many days past; but she said nothing, and they seated themselves at the table.

" And how did the ball go off yesterday evening?" said Master Walter; " I suppose it was a very grand affair?"

" It was, indeed, father; but I did not enjoy much myself."

" I suppose the rooms were hot and crowded," said her father. " Those court balls, I have heard, are generally disappointing."

" What is that noise I hear below?" said Master Walter, who, in the intervals of making a very hearty breakfast, had had his attention called to the trampling of horses in the courtyard.

" I suppose it is the pack-horses and mules, father."

" What pack-horses and mules?" inquired Master Walter, in a tone of great surprise.

" Those waiting for us. I told them to be ready to start as soon after we had finished our breakfast as possible."

Master Walter looked intensely surprised.

" Have you forgotten, father," said Bertha, " that we were to start to-morrow for Windsor?"

" Oh, nonsense!" said her father; " send directly and counter-order them; I shall not leave London."

" But remember Master Ambrose's orders, father,"

said Bertha. "He will be very angry if you disobey them."

"That was when I was ill, my dear; but I am quite well now, so send the horses away. But seriously," he continued, after Bertha had obeyed him, "my recovery has been wonderful indeed. After you left me last night I felt so unwell that I was obliged to go immediately to bed. I was so weak I could hardly walk, although I was supported on each side by a servant. When in bed I could not close my eyes, so terrible was the pain in my head. The weight of my brain seemed utterly insupportable. and it was so intensely cold it seemed to freeze me

all over. I could not get warm all I could do. I continued awake, with my hearing painfully acute, listening to every sound. At last I heard you arrive at home, and it gave me great consolation to know you had returned safely, as the night was stormy, and I thought there might have been some difficulty in finding your litter. However, you were safe, and that was a satisfaction; and I turned my head on my pillow to change my position, when the pain became so horribly acute that it was with difficulty I could restrain myself from calling for help. This continued for perhaps five minutes, when suddenly, and in an instant, the pain vanished, and I never felt better in my life. I thought I must be in a dream, and sat up in my bed to prove to myself that I was awake. The painless condition of my head continued till daybreak, and you now see me, my dear, as well as ever I was in my life."

" I am most happy, dear father, to hear it; but when did you say the pain ceased ? "

" Some few minutes after you had entered the house. I thought I heard a noise of some glass falling, and immediately the pain left me."

Bertha gazed at her father seriously for a moment, and then said, " Father, I have broken the mirror." To Bertha's great astonishment not the slightest expression of anger or curiosity appeared on her father's countenance, but he seemed to reflect deeply. Presently he said :

" Bertha, I have several times thought that my illness was in some way connected with that mirror, and now I am convinced of it. The Count told me there was a mystery attached to it, which he would some day explain to me; but unfortunately, poor man, he never had the opportunity."

"I am also convinced, dear father, that there was something magical connected with it, and although I am ashamed of the motive which induced me to break it, yet I am most happy it is broken. Some other day I will tell you the reason for my belief, if you will now excuse me; for I do not feel very well, and would wish to avoid, for the present, my confusion."

"Whenever you please, my dear," said her father, "I should be sorry to cause you annoyance in any way. I will see that the fragments are carefully picked up and thrown into the river; but I will first have an exact copy taken of those strange-looking ruby-coloured characters which were round the top of the mirror; perhaps one day we may meet with some one who can understand them, and then we may be better able to explain the mystery than we are at present."

We must now return to the history of Giles the Swineherd. It will be remembered he had increased so much in bulk that his weight was absolutely painful to him; and at the time we left him, he had much difficulty in even going through the doorway of his house. He had, nevertheless, a splendid appetite, and his fairy attendants took every care to supply him with the most dainty and succulent dishes. He was now so lazy that he would not even take the trouble to put on his own boots, and the captain of the goblins, attended by two or three assistants, waited on him every morning for that purpose. His pigs continued to be well attended to by the troop of goblins, and everything in that department had gone on in the most satisfactory manner. Capsicum waited on Giles every morning after breakfast, and gave him a correct report of all that had taken place the day before.

On the morning after the ball, Giles had remained in bed somewhat later than usual. When he awoke he was much surprised to find that neither was his breakfast ready for him, nor the fire lighted, and that neither Capsicum nor the captain of the goblins was in attendance. He waited for some time expecting them to arrive, but finding they did not make their appearance, he began to get very angry. He first called Capsicum, and when he did not come, he shouted for Calf-skin, the captain of the goblins, and for the butler, and the cook, in turn, and last of all for the faithful Rosebud. To Giles's intense disgust not one of them answered, and in a fit of passion he rolled himself out of bed, determined to explain himself in a most unmistakeable manner to all the delinquents on the subject. He hurriedly put on some clothing, and went to the door leading to the kitchen, calling aloud to his servants one after the other.

No answer having been given him, he rushed to the door, and to his great surprise saw neither the slightest vestige of kitchen nor cook. Not a furnace, not a *casserole* was to be seen; everything

was in precisely the same condition as before Giles
had made the acquaintance of the fairies.

With some difficulty, he squeezed himself through
the doorway, and proceeded to the storehouse, in
which had been improvised the sleeping apartments of the female fairies. No stout fairy housekeeper now opposed his entrance. He looked in:
not a vestige of its late tenants was to be seen in it.
The breaking of the mirror had also broken the
charm which had been placed on Giles, and he was
now again the simple swineherd, without a servant
or assistant of any kind. He now pushed through
the door lead-
ing to the pig-
sties. He cast
a glance at the
quarters of the
goblins, but
they were all
deserted like
those of the
fairies.

Giles was
puzzled what
to do, and re-
mained for
some moments

in a reverie, from which he was aroused by a
general chorus of the whole of his pigs, now
clamorous for their breakfasts. He went to the

tubs containing their food, and fortunately found they were all full. He busied himself in feeding them, an occupation which occasioned him no little fatigue, not only on account of his great bulk, but from his not having been for some time accustomed to labour. He continued at the work, however, and at last succeeded in giving them all their breakfasts.

When Giles had fed his pigs, he began to think of his own meal; but first he was under the necessity of making a fire. He collected a few sticks not particularly dry, and after experiencing some difficulty in getting into his room, he succeeded in getting his fire lighted. All this was satisfactory so far as it went, but he had now to think of what he would have for breakfast. From what he would have for breakfast his thoughts turned to what he could have, and even this presented considerable difficulty. He began to search for some provisions, but could find none, with the exception of a loaf of black bread, which had been in the house for at least a fortnight, and some potatoes from the pig stores. He put some of the latter into a saucepan with some water, and placed it on the fire. He waited impatiently, for by this time he was desperately hungry, till the potatoes were cooked, and then breakfasted, perhaps with more pleasure than he had done for some weeks past.

After breakfast Giles occupied himself in cleaning out his pig-sties, and then he worked for some hours in the garden with his spade, being fully convinced he should not see his fairy friends again. He dined and supped with a good appetite in the same frugal manner in which he had breakfasted, and that night slept sounder than he had done since his last journey to London.

He continued this mode of life for some days longer, losing some of his superabundant fat, but feeling no bad effects from the loss. One morning he received a message from the bailiff to take two hams to the house in London. He now felt no displeasure at the commission, but chose conscientiously two of the finest he could find. He started off with his load with a light heart, and arrived at the house in Bishopsgate before the hour of the servants' dinner. They received him in the kitchen with great good humour, and invited him to join them at their meal. They bantered him a good deal on his altered appearance, especially Joan the maid-servant. He in his turn joked her about the mirror, and asked her if she were not tired of looking at her face in it. After dinner  Joan inquired if the fairies had yet found him a wife, to which Giles replied that he wished to have nothing to do with fairies, and that he intended choosing a good, industrious little wife for himself.

To make a long story short, he married Joan in the end, and they made as happy a couple as could be found on the farm, or for miles round it.

Of the Mercer's Apprentice we have little to record, but that little is perfectly satisfactory. He returned to his old master in Chepe, who willingly forgave him for his temporary desertion. He lived with him for some years after his term of apprenticeship had expired, and he afterwards married the only daughter of a mercer in Barbican, and in course of time inherited the business. He lived to a good old age, and was much respected.

We must now return to Blanche de Courcelle and her Italian greyhound Fido. The reader may remember we left her in a delicate state of health, in consequence of the vexation she felt at the determination of her lover, Osmond, to go to the King's ball, where the perfidious Fido had led her to believe he intended making an offer to Bertha de Courcey. She had determined not to see him again till the ball was over, but all the persuasions of Fido could not induce her to receive his rival, old Dr. Thomas. As the day of the ball approached, Blanche's health became worse, and on the day itself she was so unwell that Osmond's mother, who called on her in the morning, was positively alarmed at the change for the worse which she noticed in the poor girl's appearance. Still Blanche determined to carry out her design of send-

ing Fido, on whom she had implicit reliance, to pass
the night at Osmond's mother's, and to bring her
intelligence the next morning of all that had passed.
She gave him especial instructions to notice in every
particular what dress Osmond wore, whether he had
purchased anything new for the occasion, and if so,
of what quality it was, and how made, what time he
left the house, in what spirits he was, and, in fact,
every circumstance respecting him.

But the directions she gave Fido as to what to
notice before Osmond's departure were few and
trifling to those he was to remark the next morning,
when he was at breakfast with his mother. Whether
he was in good or bad spirits, whether he danced
much with Bertha, and what conversations, should
he state them, passed between them; how Bertha
was dressed, whether he engaged himself to her at
the ball, at what hour he returned, and, above all,
whether he had made any appointment to meet her
again, and many other things too numerous to
mention.

Fido promised to remember them all, and to bring
her back faithful answers; but there was not the
slightest necessity for his passing the night out of
his mistress's house, for the purpose of obtaining
the information he meant to give her. As she
gave him her different instructions, he with ready
wit invented the answers he proposed to give the
next morning; all of which, it is needless to say,
were utterly false. His intended report was to state

how eager Osmond was to start for the ball, how magnificent was his dress, how his mother kissed him before he left the house, and her last instructions were to make himself as agreeable as possible to Bertha. But all these falsehoods, abominable as they were, were trifling in comparison to those he had made up in describing the conversation which would take place the next morning between mother and son at the breakfast-table. He had invented a most glowing description by Osmond of Bertha. How lovely she looked, how magnificently she - was dressed, how everybody wished to dance with her, but that she would dance with nobody but him; how at supper he had indirectly told her how much he loved her, and the kind, encouraging manner in which she received the intelligence. All these, and fifty other falsehoods, the wicked dog had prepared for the ear of his too confiding mistress.

When evening approached, Blanche called her maid, and told her to take Fido to Osmond's mother's, and to request her to keep him for the night, pleading as an excuse that, as she was much indisposed, she wished, if possible, to obtain a night's rest, but if the dog was allowed to remain in the house and were excluded from her chamber he would disturb both herself and her mother by his cries.

The girl immediately took up Fido, and proceeded to Osmond's house, where she left him, and then returned to her mistress.

Poor Blanche did not close her eyes that night.

She pictured to herself everything as she imagined
it would occur, and cried over the supposed offer
Osmond would make to Bertha, until she was afraid
her mother would the next day notice the inflamed
state of her eyes.

The next morning, about eleven o'clock, Blanche
sent her maid for the dog, after having sent to her
mother a message that she should keep her room
all the morning. About noon the girl returned
with Fido, who seemed delighted to see his mistress,
and instantly leaped on her bed, with every sign of
pleasure.

Blanche now requested the girl to leave the room,
and as soon as the door was closed she took her dog
in her arms, and addressed him with—

" Dear Fido, now tell me truthfully everything
that occurred."

The only notice that Fido took of her request was
simply to lick her face.

" Now do not be silly, but tell me at once like a
good dog," said Blanche, but she received no more
satisfactory reply than before.

" Fido," said Blanche, " if you do not answer
me directly, I shall get very angry with you." Still
she received no reply. Blanche now really got very
angry at the dog's disobedience, and gave him a
smart tap on his shoulder, which he took in play and
immediately leaped from her arms on the foot of the
bed, and commenced barking at her.

Blanche now fairly lost her temper, and taking her

dog by the neck gave him several sharp blows on the sides.   This he by no means approved of, and set his

teeth so sharply in her hand as to make the blood flow somewhat freely.   Blanche got frightened, and screamed loudly for her maid, who, on entering the room and finding her mistress wounded, inquired the cause.   On hearing that the dog had bitten her, she instantly seized him and inflicted on him a very different kind of castigation from that which he had received from his mistress.   Fido howled fearfully under his punishment, but not a word did he say, and Blanche ordered him to be taken away and placed in a dark closet, there to remain till he had recovered his temper.

Poor Blanche now passed some hours in great grief and anxiety, but in the afternoon her maid knocked at her door and told her that Osmond's mother had arrived and wished to see her, as she was much concerned about her health.   Blanche instantly ordered her to be admitted, and shortly afterwards the old lady entered the room.   She kissed Blanche very affectionately, and inquired, with evident sympathy in her tone, if she were better.   Blanche replied that she felt more at ease, which was utterly untrue, as she was at that moment labouring under the most cruel curiosity.

Osmond's mother now seated herself beside Blanche's bed, and the conversation turned on ordinary topics, till Blanche's anxiety could allow her to remain no longer in doubt, and she inquired what news her friend had heard of the King's ball.

"None whatever, my dear," was the reply.

Blanche was for a moment silent, and she then asked after Osmond.

"I have not seen him this morning, my dear. He left the house for business before I was up."

"That was very diligent of him," said Blanche, "after all the fatigue he must have had last night."

"What fatigue, my dear?"

"At the ball, I mean," said Blanche.

"Oh, he did not go after all."

"Not go?" said Blanche; 'why I understood he had set his heart upon going, and that he had ordered a new suit of clothes for the occasion."

"That is perfectly true," said Osmond's mother, "and he came home from business early yesterday for the purpose of being at the ball in good time; but when I told him how ill you appeared when I called on you in the afternoon, he was so much hurt that he said he could not enjoy himself if he went, and he remained at home with me all the evening."

Blanche was for some moments silent and conscience-stricken, for she perceived she had been guilty of a gross injustice towards her lover. She then said:

" I am very sorry he has been disappointed on my account, and I shall thank him for his kind feeling when I see him."

" You might have had an opportunity of doing so this evening if you had been better, for he is to call and escort me home."

" I feel so much stronger to-day," said Blanche, " that I think I shall get up."

Osmond's mother now left the room, and Blanche dressed herself, by no means hastily; perhaps she had never taken greater pains with her toilette than she did that afternoon. Osmond called for his mother as agreed, and Blanche received him in a most friendly manner. Nothing afterwards occurred to mar their courtship. Blanche's mother soon afterwards withdrew all opposition to the match, and the couple were married the next year in the parish church of St. Mary's, Newington. Unfortunately from that time the author, although indefatigable in his researches, has been unable to find any record of them; but from the amiable characters of both, it is more than probable they lived happily together. Fido, it should be remarked, never recovered the use of his speech.

Of the Sacristan we have little to tell. He soon quitted his church duties and married the widow, on Kennington Common. He carried on the business of a market gardener, having a stall in the Borough Market. He was a good, affectionate, and obedient husband in all things but one. No persuasion on the part of his wife could induce him to keep pigs, although she argued, and with reason, that with the great quantity of refuse vegetables they had at their disposal, pigs would prove a most lucrative investment.

The Lord Mayor's sister remained for some time in a state of great anxiety after her adventure, fearing the king of the beggars might again call on her; but at last she heard that that worthy had been hung for what the law termed murder, but what his immediate subjects attributed to the hardness of the times. Of the Ring of Frastrada nothing certain is known. A ring somewhat resembling it in shape and antiquity was seen about two years since in a marine-store dealer's shop in Ratcliffe Highway; but if it were the same its virtues  had entirely vanished, for the proprietress had long endeavoured to obtain the goodwill of the police but without effect. They were perpetually accusing her of receiving stolen goods, and persecuting her "shameful."

Of the Physician and his Wife we have already spoken, and there remain but two persons for us to mention—the Merchant and his Daughter. The latter changed greatly for the better, both in temper and manner, after the King's ball. She married a young and wealthy merchant, made an excellent wife and mother, and lived to see her eldest son elected Lord Mayor of London. • Master Walter died at a good old age much respected. One subject, however, to the last gave him much anxiety and annoyance. He was never able to obtain the meaning of the characters on the mirror. He got them faithfully copied, and we now present them to our readers in the fervent hope that some one at last may be found who can translate them.

www.ingramcontent.com/pod-product-compliance
Lightning Source LLC
Chambersburg PA
CBHW020852020726
47497CB00005B/1367